Wagaya wa Kakuriyo no kashihonya san Novel 1
©Shinobumaru (Story)
This edition originally published in Japan in 2019 by
MICRO MAGAZINE, INC., Tokyo.
English translation rights arranged with
MICRO MAGAZINE, INC., Tokyo.

Seven Seas press and purchase enquiries can be sent to
Marketing Manager Lianne Sentar at press@gomanga.com.
Information regarding the distribution and purchase of
digital editions is available from Digital Manager CK Russell
at digital@gomanga.com.

Follow Seven Seas Entertainment online at
sevenseasentertainment.com.

TRANSLATION: Jason Muell
ADAPTATION: Michelle McGuinness
COVER DESIGN: Nicky Lim
LOGO DESIGN: George Panella
INTERIOR LAYOUT & DESIGN: Clay Gardner
COPY EDITOR: Jade Gardner
PROOFREADER: Meg van Huygen
LIGHT NOVEL EDITOR: E.M. Candon
PREPRESS TECHNICIAN: Rhiannon Rasmussen-Silverstein
PRODUCTION MANAGER: Lissa Pattillo
MANAGING EDITOR: Julie Davis
ASSOCIATE PUBLISHER: Adam Arnold
PUBLISHER: Jason DeAngelis

ISBN: 978-1-64827-622-4
Printed in Canada
First Printing: October 2021
10 9 8 7 6 5 4 3 2 1

THE HAUNTED BOOKSTORE

Gateway to a Parallel Universe

VOLUME 1

The Spirit Daughter and the Exorcist Son

WRITTEN BY

Shinobumaru

TRANSLATED BY

Jason Muell

Airship

Seven Seas Entertainment

TABLE OF Contents

A Peculiar Girl in the Land of Spirits

AT THE END of an unremarkable back alley stood a holy tree. From the base of that tree, one could catch a glimpse of a large mirror mounted just within a shrine.

A world entirely different from our own lurked just beyond the glass.

The line separating the human world from the spirit realm is quite hazy—so hazy that people can easily lose their way and stumble into great danger. Every person—every thing, really—living in the spirit realm is some kind of monster. Any person unlucky enough to tumble into that realm of sunless darkness has to fight for their life against throngs of spirits eager to eat them alive. How do I know this? I'm Muramoto Kaori, and I was raised in the spirit realm.

Yes, I'm a human. One day, when I was around three years old, I wandered away from my parents and found myself there. A peculiar spirit took me in and cared for me—a *very* peculiar spirit. You see, children are a real delicacy in these parts.

"I've got something intriguing for a man of such interests," I said.

I checked the paper bag in my hand one last time before hurrying to the station. Seeing my prize put a spring in my step as I made my way through a city painted by an auburn sunset. Everyone around me looked to be in high spirits; it seemed I wasn't the only one enjoying the weight of my purse after payday.

I hopped on my train to make my way home. After one transfer, I stepped off in the middle of a run-of-the-mill residential area. The sunset had dimmed to twilight; lights winked on in the homes and buildings lining the street while the wafting scent of curry and other dinners sent my stomach grumbling. But no one paid me the least bit of mind as I passed all of this and stopped at an old deity watching over the roadside. The usual offerings of flowers decorated the red-bibbed deity. Quite fashionable, in my opinion.

This little Buddhist statue was a Dosojin, connected to the local folk beliefs. Positioned at intersections and right in the center of town, Dosojin warded off any evil spirits trying to sneak into the neighborhood while also promoting the health and prosperity of the local children. Nowadays, however, most people just walked past them without a second glance. In fact, I remembered hearing that it was mostly old people who took care of the little guys now. Perhaps it was just their fate to slowly fade away as time moved on.

Alas, that would be a bit of a problem for me. You see, these statues served as beacons to help me find my way home. I scanned the road to ensure I was alone before resting my hand atop the small shrine in which the statue sat.

"Back home," I said.

The world instantly darkened, the sky slowly fading from lovely orange to black. Stars brightened the dark, too many to count, while waves of red, blue, and green washed through the sky in waving auroras. This was the sky of the spirit realm, the land of the dead, a world of perpetual night. That humble roadside deity stood guard over the very portal separating the human world from this one.

"Welcome back."

I searched for the source of the voice until I found an adorable figure perched atop the shrine.

"Oh, Nyaa-san! I'm back," I said with a smile.

The black cat lazing on top of the shrine stretched luxuriously, wagged her three tails, and gazed up at me with large, round eyes. "Well, somebody's late today."

I'd known Nyaa-san since we were both little, and it was her habit to wait for me to return every time I left the spirit realm. She could be a bit direct, but that was only because she was something of a worrywart—and my best friend.

"Well, it's the busy period right now," I said. "They're working me to the bone."

"Well, shouldn't you just quit, then?" Nyaa-san asked. "Instead, you could just sit around and pet me all day long. See? That's a pretty good idea. We should do that."

What a cat-like way of thinking. I couldn't help but laugh.

"No can do. I'm working in the human world because I need money."

"Huh, sounds annoying."

I chuckled. "Working is actually a lot more fun than you'd think."

"Hmm...well, I guess if you're okay with it, then that's fine."

Nyaa-san hopped down and padded toward town. As I followed, I caught a whiff of the prize nestled in my paper bag. Oh, she was probably so impatient waiting for this particular gift! I smirked as I ran to catch up with Nyaa-san.

Side by side, we approached a town—yes, the spirit realm had towns. They were a bit old and mysterious, but undeniably beautiful at the same time.

The majority of the buildings were made of wood. The rusty signs dangling precariously before shops had names handwritten in kanji and katakana, like something out of a bygone era. There were the usual places like the Greengrocer and Butcher, as well as more dubious shops such as Eyeball Emporium and Flesh 'R' Us.

As we walked, lights from behind barred windows splashed into the street and voices spilled out from within shops. On the larger streets, we joined a crush of beings and savvy salesmen trying to pluck out customers from the throng. Alongside the usual wares, like fresh fruit and vegetables, we saw a wide variety of spirit realm-specific goods such as spirits shrieking unearthly cries, strange medicines, and clothes embroidered with ominous symbols.

Though the town was gas powered, the light glowing from every home and storefront didn't come from burning fuel as it would in the human world. Here, we put little butterflies called glimmerflies into the glass bulbs that lit both streets and houses.

The glimmerfly, a ghostly butterfly particular to this realm, got its name from the scales on its wings and body. As it fluttered about, those scales cast a mystical glow, but sadly, the little creature would eventually burn out and fade. We always needed to gather more of them in order to keep the lanterns going, hence the need for butterfly hunters. These folks stalked the town with bamboo baskets brimming with butterflies, and they were a classic feature of the spirit realm's landscape.

But the glimmerflies were special for more than just their ability to glow.

"Glad to see you back, Kaori-chan. I see you're still quite popular with the glimmerflies," a snake-haired woman called out.

"Well, it's pretty nice to not need a lamp," I admitted.

A flurry of glimmerflies clustered nearby, but they avoided the woman in favor of me. You see, they seemed to prefer humans.

I was certainly a sight to behold in the spirit town as I strolled through with a glimmerfly swarm fluttering around me. These days, it made me more approachable to the supernatural beings inhabiting this realm, but I had actually hated glimmerflies as a kid. Whenever they swarmed around me, it had reminded me that I was a stranger to this realm. As a child I had sobbed, thrashing at the little bugs, trying to push them away so they would stop marking me out as different—as other. It had been bad enough knowing I didn't really belong; I didn't need a constant glowing reminder.

But that had been a long time ago. Now I was grown up, and they no longer bothered me. In fact, the glimmerflies served as a convenient light source. Once I'd learned to deal with them, I could finally appreciate them for their beauty.

A woman with a face devoid of any features called out to me. "Hi, Strangeling. I'll be by later to drop off some vegetables, so leave your door open, 'kay?"

She ran a Japanese confectionery shop so well known for its delicious treats that a line formed outside it first thing in the morning every day. I was still always the first one who got to sample her latest creations.

"Wow, that's great! Thanks!" I called back.

"Swing on by sometime this weekend, Kaori-chan. I've got a new treat I'd like you to try."

Nyaa-san perked up. "Oooh! I'm coming too!"

"Oh, this is for you, Strangeling," another supernatural well-wisher said.

"For me? Thank you."

I'd hardly made any progress down the road and already my arms were full of gifts. I had to jog to catch up with Nyaa-san, who waited patiently for me farther down the street.

"Looks like you've scored again," Nyaa-san said. "Not bad."

Even with all these gifts, we didn't linger. Even though I was more or less accepted in town as the "Strangeling," the spirit realm could be a dangerous place for humans. Thankfully, the local spirits regularly showered me with kindness—a side humans rarely ever saw.

"Myaaao."

Nyaa-san mewed as we reached the end of the road, where a two-story wooden house that had certainly seen better days awaited us. Part of the first floor was dedicated to a retail space, marked by the decrepit wooden sign that clung desperately to the wall: "Book Rentals." This was my home, the one and only bookstore in the entire spirit realm.

I slid the glass door open and called out, "I'm hooooome!"

The glimmerflies scattered as the smell of incense hit my nose. I flung the door wide and stepped into the shop. The creak of the floorboards transported me to yet another world—one where I was home.

The room wasn't big by any means, only around sixteen square meters or so. The bookshelves covering the walls stood so tall, you couldn't see their tops. Several old battle-scarred ladders leaned against the shelves. Glimmerfly bulbs dangled about the room, attempting to illuminate bookshelves that had gone amber with age. The bright spines of the books jammed on those shelves seemed to float in the dim lighting, almost as if they were hovering around the shop.

Mysteries abounded within the spirit realm's only bookstore. For one thing, the ceiling loomed far higher than seemed possible from the outside. First-time visitors often gawked at the height of the shelves. Obviously, this implied the shop had more than one floor, and while there was a stairwell in the main house, sometimes you could find yourself on the second floor without climbing a single step. Moreover, no matter how packed those shelves became, we never ran out of space for more books.

How did it all work? Well, if the shop owner knew, he certainly wasn't telling. Trade secrets, you know?

I called out again as I passed the bookshelf dedicated to new releases, which was placed smack-dab in the middle of the main room. "Hey, you asleep? I said I'm hoooooome!"

A thin, raspy voice finally answered. "Oh, you're back."

As I slid open the door connecting the store to the main house, my gaze fell on a man lying on the tatami flooring—my adoptive father, the very "peculiar" spirit who'd taken me in as a child.

An older man, around his mid-forties or so, he usually wore a stern expression that was easily undermined by his sleepy gaze and unkempt facial hair. When silent, he scowled, and when talking, he wore a perpetual look of disappointment, a lifelong habit as far as I could tell. In short, he was pretty much like any other middle-aged man. Only the two horns sticking out of his forehead and the light scale pattern covering his skin indicated that he wasn't human.

I sighed and started to gather up the papers scattered across the floor. Glancing over at his tea table, I found the rest of his manuscript beside his uneaten lunch.

"Really, Shinonome-san?" I asked. "Looks like you got too into your writing and forgot to eat again. Listen, if you're going to get so hungry that you pass out like this, you really should just eat. You're going to get sick one of these days, you know."

"Well, you were going to come back home sooner or later, so I figured we could just eat together," he grumbled. Shinonome-san didn't even bother to turn toward me as he spoke, running his long nails through his graying hair.

All I could do was sigh again. Here he was, wearing his best yukata, and now it was thoroughly wrinkled from his floor nap. Flashes of pale flesh peeked out from the rumpled folds.

Day in and day out, I was always chastising him for his careless behavior, but nothing ever changed. He just couldn't wrap his mind around the fact that I wanted a father figure who at least pretended to care about how he presented himself.

"Come on, grow up and stop being so shabby!" I moaned.

As per usual, Shinonome-san just waved his hand as if he were dismissing a bothersome fly. "I don't get what all the screeching's about. And I have no idea how you managed to grow up like this, considering how I raised you. Now, why don't you just go get married and get out of my hair, you twit?"

"I'll do no such thing until you finally learn how to take care of yourself," I sniffed. "Just imagine if I came back here to have my first baby and had to show off a feeble old man for a dad. No thanks."

"Harrumph." Apparently, this struck a nerve, because he snatched up the rice ball from his lunch and started chomping on it.

"I'm making your favorite for dinner tonight: fried minced cutlets," I sang. "If you don't hurry and clean up this mess, I'm just going to have to eat them all by myself."

"Really?" he choked, eyes flashing. "And...any alcohol?"

"I've got that, too, but just one bottle."

"Fantastic!"

He chuckled ruefully, though he did finally start to clean. I tied on an apron and left him to it, turning toward the kitchen. Just as I was about to step out, though, a huge ball of yarn bounced past my feet.

"Watch out, Nyaa-san! I could've tripped," I cried.

"Any fish for me?" Nyaa-san asked. She blinked up at me with large, bright eyes. She was usually a sleepy creature, so the effect of those twinkling eyes was not insignificant—they always made me feel a twinge of jealousy.

"Of course!"

A low growl reverberated deep in Nyaa-san's throat like some kind of laugh. "Well, that's good then." She padded to the corner, snagged her toy in her teeth, and proudly carried it over.

At last, I'd gotten the whole, weird family together. Sighing with exhaustion, I rolled up my sleeves and headed to the kitchen.

I oven-fried the cutlets in the toaster oven until they were nice and crunchy before plating them with some potato salad and cherry tomatoes. I added bowls of freshly cooked rice, some sea-weed and miso soup, and a pickled vegetable I'd recently found. Finally, I set down a bottle of beer for Shinonome-san.

"Huh, not bad," I mused.

The minced cutlets were pretty big and made from Japanese beef, a delicacy we hardly could have afforded were it not my payday. I figured they'd be perfect covered in sauce with a bit of mustard. As I carried them to the living room, I heard Shinonome-san meeting a guest in the shop.

"Hello," said Shinonome-san.

"Ah, uh...yes. Hi," mumbled the guest.

The guest, Goblin, bowed his horned head when he noticed my arrival. It wasn't too unusual for us to receive a customer so late in the day. The spirit realm didn't have much in the way of entertainment, which made our bookstore fantastically popular. The spirits here could get their hands on various sundry items from the human realm, including books and other entertainment, but those kinds of things came in limited quantity and at a high price, all of which contributed to the popularity of our little bookshop on the outskirts of town.

"Well?" Judging by Shinonome-san's perplexed expression, something was amiss. "What, don't have enough? This is already heavily discounted, you know."

"W-would this cover it?" Goblin desperately reached into his pocket and pulled out some colored pebbles from a riverbank.

"Sorry. I can't just rent out my books for some pretty rocks."

Goblin visibly wilted. He likely lived far out in the mountains, in a place where money had little worth. Like many of our customers, he'd arrived with few coins to his name.

Shinonome-san scowled as he studied the dejected Goblin. He scratched his face and took a long draw from his smoking pipe. "All right then," he conceded, "if you tell me the most interesting experience you've had, I'll consider you paid up. How does that sound? All you have to do is talk and you can borrow a book. Not a bad offer, I'd say."

Goblin brightened and cheerfully launched into his story. Shortly thereafter, he hurried away with a book of fairy tales hugged against his chest.

"Do you really think a story about someone's loincloth getting washed down the river will sell for anything?" I asked.

Shinonome-san huffed as he scrawled the story we'd just heard into his notebook. "Hard to say."

This was one reason why we were poor. If we'd lived out in the mountains like Goblin, we'd have no need for money. But living in a home just outside a busy shopping distinct instead didn't come cheap. Despite that, Shinonome-san often cut deals like this, further eating into our profits. If only he charged all our customers, we'd have more than enough for the two of us to live on. Instead, I had no choice but to go out and work a part-time job in the human world to make ends meet.

Alas, there was just no getting around the continuous flow of penniless mountain spirits who came down here yearning for books. As the daughter of a bookstore owner, I was an avid reader myself and also wanted to help get books into the hands of as many people as possible, so I sympathized, but it didn't make our situation any easier to manage.

As we stood there in silence, our shoulders slumped in unison, and Shinonome-san finally spoke up. "...I guess dinner's gone cold, huh?"

"Want me to reheat the cutlets?"

"No, it's fine. They'll get too dry if you do."

"That's true."

Just as we finally sat down to eat, a commotion sounded outside. What now?

"What's going on out there?" I asked. A spirit-related incident wasn't exactly rare around these parts. I glanced out at the road running past the shop, figuring someone must be kicking up a fuss as usual. Right as I looked outside, a rush of air blasted past, and a flurry of glimmerflies darted off toward something.

"Well, that's strange," I murmured, "seeing a flurry of glimmerflies like that." My heart began to race. Of all the strange things I'd seen in the spirit realm, this was entirely new.

I turned back to Shinonome-san, hoping he might know something. But before I even had a chance to ask, he was charging outside, wooden sandals in hand.

"I'll be back!" he called. He hopped back and forth from one foot to the next before he finally slipped on his sandals and took off at a run, holding the edge of his yukata up and out of the way.

"Hey, wait up! What's going on?!" I shouted.

"Nothing to worry about, Kaori! Just stay inside!"

"No way!"

"Waugh!"

My vehement refusal distracted Shinonome-san just enough that he stumbled. He took a few more wobbly steps forward before spinning around to face me. "Why?! I told you to stay inside! Who knows what dangers might be out here?"

"Fine by me! I'll bring Nyaa-san. No problem!"

Nyaa-san was conveniently already padding around by my feet, so I reached down and grabbed her by the scruff of her neck.

"Nyaoo!" She let out a screech, but I didn't have time to concern myself with her dignity.

"Just stop it and listen to me for once, you twit!" Shinonome-san howled.

"I don't see what the big deal is! You're just an overprotective old man!"

"Gaah! Where did I go wrong raising you, huh?"

"Oh, shush!"

I shoved my shoes on and dashed outside, but by the time I got there, Shinonome-san was already gone.

"Are you really going, Kaori?" Nyaa-san asked. Those big eyes were all worry this time.

"Sorry, but I have a bad feeling about this." I shoved my anxiety aside and rushed ahead. I couldn't shake the image of the glimmerflies. I knew of only one thing that could attract a swarm like that...

I skidded to a stop on the main road where the glimmerflies flitted frantically. My eyes darted everywhere, searching for Shinonome-san, but I couldn't see him through the thick veil of beating glimmerfly wings. There was just no way I'd be able to find him in this.

"Shinonome-san, where are you?!" I called.

Before the words had even left my mouth, a fat droplet splashed to the ground. The rain rapidly intensified and, one by one, the glimmerflies fled the watery onslaught.

There!

As the curtain of glowing insects dispersed, I finally caught sight of Shinonome-san. Relief washed over me, but it only lasted a split second before cold dread rushed through my veins to replace it.

The glimmerflies fluttered about, illuminating the dark, gloomy world of the spirit realm.

My father stood among them, drenched in rain.

At his feet lay a boy with white hair, sprawled on his side with blood oozing out of his wounds. A *human* boy.

CHAPTER 1

The Oboke Recluse

THE RAIN DRUMMED DOWN outside the window, blocking what little light this realm of perpetual night received. Hence our heavy reliance on glimmerflies. Two insect-powered lamps lit the room now, casting eerie, uneven glows.

"This looks disgusting..." the boy said, scowling at the bowl he shoved back at me. "I only eat the highest-quality organic rice, cooked in a clay pot." He turned away with a huff but glanced back at me from the corner of his eye. "Hey, why are you looking at me like that? Is this how you treat injured patients?"

"I think it's a perfectly acceptable look for people who barge into someone else's house and put on airs—like you," I said. "Besides, you sure look to be in pretty good spirits. I hardly think you need taking care of."

I poured the uneaten rice porridge back into the pot and glared at the boy.

He called himself Shirai Suimei. He was pale everywhere, from skin with hardly any pigment to his shock of white hair, though he did have brown eyes. The overall effect was still like one of those somber pretty boys from a manga.

"Of course I need to be taken care of. Can't you see I'm injured?" Though that haughty tone certainly didn't fit the pretty boy image.

Okay, fine. Suimei was actually as injured as he claimed. A bandage covered the cut on his forehead. The wound wasn't deep, but it had bled a ton, like head wounds tend to do.

That's right, he was still a victim in all this, so I needed to be nice. It had already occurred to me that his arrogance might be his way of masking some sort of mental distress. My shoulders slumped as I thought of Shinonome-san, the person who'd first taught me that lesson.

"All right, looks like I don't have much of a choice," I sighed. "I'll be looking after you, but the moment you're better, I want you out. Human."

"Huh?" Suimei narrowed his eyes to examine me. "But you're human too, lady. What're you doing here?"

"I don't need to explain myself to you."

I turned my back on my self-proclaimed patient and headed for the kitchen, mind wandering back to how this had all come to be my problem...

It had started the night before, in fact.

The rain pounded down, soaking through my clothes, making

them cling to my skin. I wanted to pluck the wet fabric away, but there was no time for that.

I looked at my father in horror. He stood frozen amid the downpour.

"It looks like you killed him..." I trailed off.

"I did no such thing, that much I can promise," Shinonome-san insisted.

"Fair enough. I doubt you even could."

"Oh, shut up, you!"

"So, you going to fess up?"

"I told you, that's not what happened, so there's nothing for me to fess up *to*. This isn't the human world, you know. There won't be any police to come looking for the culprit. Idiot. And—hey, didn't I tell you not to follow me?" Shinonome-san covered his face with his hands and tilted his head up toward the sky.

Ah well, might as well stop teasing him already. I set Nyaa-san down so I could kneel at the boy's side. His eyes, lined with white lashes, were squeezed shut. He wouldn't be waking up any time soon. The pouring rain washed away the blood oozing from his forehead, dyeing the ground beneath him red.

"Is he alive?" Shinonome-san asked.

"Yes, it seems like he's just unconscious. Despite how the bleeding makes it look, his injury isn't all that bad."

Even with the rain, some of the glimmerflies stubbornly lingered, their light illuminating the boy's face. His forehead was cold to the touch, though that might have been due to the rain. In any case, we couldn't leave him here; his condition would surely worsen. Given the bleeding, it might even prove fatal. We needed to move him indoors, and fast.

Besides, judging by the swarming glimmerflies, he was definitely human.

"Someone's going to eat him if we just leave him here," I said. "We've gotta do something, right?"

The denizens of the town were starting to take notice of the unusual glimmerfly swarm. It wouldn't be long before spirits of all shapes and sizes were drawn to this place, and they'd no doubt be quite pleased to find an unconscious human just waiting for them.

"Kaori?"

For some reason, my whole body was trembling.

Even though I didn't have any real memories of when I'd entered the spirit realm, just the thought of this boy getting lost and winding up here suddenly filled me with despair.

Then Shinonome-san wrapped his arms around me. My father's gentle warmth transferred through his large palms and into me, slowly easing my anxiety. As long as I had this peculiar spirit by my side, I knew I'd be fine.

Nyaa-san finally broke the silence. "So whaddya wanna do, Kaori? You're gonna take him back to his world, right?"

I knew it would be wise to heed her suggestion. All we had to do was get him to an ambulance. Medical professionals would whisk him off to a hospital where he could be reunited with his family. In fact, I could leave as soon as the ambulance arrived. I was very much on board with this idea and was just about to agree when a hand grabbed me.

"Aaahh..." The unconscious boy finally woke up. "Don't... leave me. Stay...here..."

A feverish flush lit his cheeks. His brown eyes gazed right through me. Immediately after muttering his plea, he fell back into unconsciousness. He was like a sickly child reaching for his mother. Oh, no...

"Haaah, we can't just leave the kid here like this." Shinonome-san shook his head. He hefted Suimei over his shoulder.

"Shinonome-san?!" I gasped.

All he offered was a noncommittal shrug. "Remember when you were young? No matter how tiny the spirit, how weak the animal, you could never turn your back on them. Well, that's the same here. Damn." He shot me a teasing grin. "I guess the blame falls on whoever raised their kid like that, huh? You gotta be ready to take responsibility."

With that, we made our slow way down the street, the boy slung over Shinonome-san's shoulder. He'd be coming home with us after all. The idea prodded at some strange, dark memories deep within me, but what else could we do?

"Thanks," I muttered along the way.

"It's nothing, really," Shinonome-san said. "Oh, but hey, you could pay me back by making meat for dinner tomorrow! Something big, thick, and juicy that practically falls right off the plate."

That stopped me right in my tracks. He had to be joking, right? "You know we can't afford that."

Shinonome-san just marched cheerfully on ahead, not a care in the world.

"Nnng...gah! That irresponsible little..." I grumbled. Despite my frustration, the familiar banter set me at ease. Jeez, he knew just how to get to me. In the end, Shinonome-san was a great dad.

I watched him carry Suimei ahead of me and smiled to myself, knowing that despite it all, I really could rely on him.

"It figures he'd finally give in," I sighed to myself.

Despite his earlier protests, Suimei eventually caved in to hunger and requested food. With no shortage of annoyance, I served him another helping of rice porridge and watched him completely clean his bowl. Perhaps he'd finally learned a little humility and gratitude for our efforts in his rescue and care.

"It was certainly edible," he said.

Ungrateful brat. I wrung out his clothes with a bit more force than strictly necessary. "Gaaaah, this has to be some kind of scam!" I groaned. "Any normal person would have said thank you by now, you know? Maybe mentioned how they'll never forget the favor—something like that, right?!"

"Heh, and what kind of favor are you talking about?" he asked.

"Oh shush, you. Hurry up and change your clothes."

"I was going to do that anyway."

What had happened to the weak, helpless boy sprawled in the street with a head wound? He's become quite the brazen little interloper. He'd looked on the verge of death when we found him, but apparently we had nothing to worry about.

"I guess it's a positive thing that you're feeling so self-possessed," I muttered.

Suimei didn't respond as I shoved his clothes toward him and left the room. I hadn't seen my father for some time, so I headed to see if he'd come home yet. Shortly after dropping off Suimei, Shinonome-san had left the house, and he still hadn't returned. According to the clock, it'd been almost a full day. Just where had he run off to?

"I swear, I won't forgive him if he's out playing at a time like this," I moaned.

Suddenly, a commotion sounded in the store. I hurried toward the noise, assuming Shinonome-san had finally returned. Yet all that awaited me was Goblin.

"G-good evening..." Goblin's eyes darted around uneasily before he peered toward our home. Maybe he was here to see Shinonome-san? Well, he seemed a harmless sort, so I knelt down to meet him at eye level.

"What's wrong?" I asked. "Did something happen? Unfortunately, the proprietor isn't here right now."

"R-really?!" Goblin sat down hard on the ground as if in shock, and thick tears trailed down his cheeks. In the following instant, he lost the last of his composure.

Pushing a poor little guy like him would only make matters worse, so I kept my face as flat and calm as possible as I reached out to comfort him.

"What...?" he mumbled. Goblin tensed as I ran my hand through his straw-like hair. I didn't push him for answers, just waited patiently until he was ready. Finally, he opened his mouth. "I-I-I visited my friend to see if he'd read me that book I borrowed. B-but he's in real bad shape. Like, in real bad pain. I-I just don't know what to do."

"So you came here?" I asked.

Goblin nodded stiffly and began to sob all over again.

"Thank you for telling me. You did a good job." I pulled him into a tight embrace. He shuddered, clinging tightly to my clothes with his crimson hands. He seemed badly rattled by whatever had happened to his friend. What a heavy burden to carry all on his own. Shinonome-san might have been able to help, but he was nowhere to be found at the moment. "What's your friend's name?" I asked gently.

His voice trembled as he spoke. "Y-Yamajiji."

"Yamajiji" was a legendary spirit said to live deep in the mountains of Kochi Prefecture on the island of Shikoku. Much like the Yamauba, he was believed to be incredibly wealthy and would often challenge hunters to contests to see who could yell the loudest.

Many spirits out in the spirit realm didn't have their own unique name, so we usually resorted to using locations to figure out who someone was talking about. "Yamajiji? Where's he from?" I asked.

"Huh? Uh, I...uh...well...O-O-O-Oboke."

"Oh! Right!" I smacked my fist against my palm. I actually knew the Oboke Yamajiji.

I got some details on Yamajiji's condition from Goblin, and

then I started preparing. It sounded like the usual issue. I stowed a box of medicine in my bag and looked up to find Suimei watching me, but I ignored him for the moment.

Aaaaand...done! I hefted the bag onto my back and reached out for Goblin's hand. "All right, ready to go, Goblin-kun?"

"Huh? You're coming with me?" he asked.

"Of course. Just leave it to me!" I thumped my chest several times for emphasis and smiled down at Goblin.

I clasped his hand, and we stepped out into town. Fortunately, the rain had finally let up, returning the world to its usual rainbow-sheened darkness. Goblin kept glancing up at me nervously as we walked, but I smiled and gestured at the sky. "Hey, look."

"W-wow! So many glimmerflies!" he gasped.

"Pretty cool, huh?"

Before I knew it, the insects surrounded us. Most spirits marveled at the sight of a human standing in a glowing cloud of glimmerflies, and Goblin proved no different. His eyes practically shimmered as he reached out for the bugs.

"Having fun?" I asked.

"Yeah!"

I smiled. Poor Goblin was finally relaxing enough to enjoy himself. It seemed these glimmerflies could be useful for something other than illumination, huh? *Thanks, guys.*

One landed right on my finger, almost as if in response to my unspoken praise. "Oh, hey there."

All the illumination jogged my memory. I reached into my pocket and pulled out a folded piece of paper, inside of which were two stars: one yellow and the other a pale pink. I tossed one into my mouth and the other into Goblin's. The star melted away within the warm confines of my mouth, a sweet, sugary mixture seeping over my tongue. The faceless woman from the confectionery shop, Noppera-bo, often made these as a specialty item, and Shinonome-san always bought some for me.

("Hey, you listening?" someone grumbled.)

Surprise flashed over Goblin's face when I popped the candy into his mouth, but in the next moment, his cheeks flushed a bright red and a look of sheer bliss washed across his face. He pressed his crimson hands against his cheeks and let out a contented sigh. "This must be what happiness tastes like!"

Looks like that sweet little star candy managed to wipe away all his concerns. I had to admit, his reaction was absolutely adorable.

"Don't ignore me," someone growled.

"Ehhh?" I seized up as someone grabbed my collar and yanked me back. Spinning around, I found Suimei staring blankly back at me.

"What, you wanted some too?" I asked.

"No." He looked supremely annoyed.

"Then go back home and rest," I said. "You're a helpless patient in need of diligent nursing, aren't you?"

At this, Suimei stuck out his lip. "What, and sit idly by while the person who saved my life puts themself in harm's way?"

Suimei reached out and clung to my arm. I blinked. Admittedly, there was something handsome about that stoic, emotionless face of his. His voice was always unusually calm and level. Yet now his eyes wavered, revealing his worry. Apparently he really was concerned about my well-being.

"You know, I'm surprised you're such a nice guy," I said.

Suimei furrowed his brow. "Surprised is a little rude, I think. You know, unlike the Yamauba, Yamajiji isn't really known for attacking humans, though he's no stranger to abducting children and cattle. I really don't think an ordinary girl like you is in any position to try to meet with him."

I snorted and held his gaze while I called out to Nyaa-san. "Hey, are people back in the human world usually this familiar with the spirit realm as this guy?"

"Hard to say," Nyaa-san said. "I spent a lot of time out there, and I didn't really meet all that many people who were so well informed. There were some, of course, but they were usually hobbyists, researchers, authors...and exorcists."

Suimei's eyes widened. For all he tried to hide his emotions, he was basically an open book. His eyes revealed everything he tried to hold back.

A sly smirk tugged on my lips, and my hand fell on his shoulder with a thump. I leaned in and whispered into his ear. "I have no idea what brought you here to the spirit realm, but this is no place for humans. I'm sure it's a bit strange for you to hear that coming from me, but all the same, assuming you *are* an exorcist, then you must know how dangerous these spirits can be."

He remained silent.

"I'm just trying to do you a favor...and thank you for worrying about me. But you best go home before one of the spirits out here decides to chomp your head right off."

It was a dire warning, but that really was just how things went in the spirit realm. Though special circumstances allowed me to remain, any other human could hardly hope to survive for long.

Suimei brushed my hand away and glowered at the ground, a despondent look creasing his face. "I already know all that. But...I have no home to go back to. It's not like I came here without a reason. I just messed up and got hurt. That's why I can't return."

"Hmm." Messed up? What did that mean? And what did it have to do with finding him lying in the street bleeding?

I narrowed my eyes at the strange boy. He looked young. Not only that, he was even shorter than me. Probably a high school student.

And how did some kid become an exorcist? Wasn't that a job for adults? The one time I'd seen an exorcist was when an old man had come here to try to face off with some spirits. He'd been covered in inexplicable amulets and stones. But Suimei was slight and small, hardly intimidating. Maybe he was some kind of exorcist in training? In that case, maybe I could work with him.

I chuckled to myself as the plan fell into place. Suimei's face tensed while Nyaa-san grimaced.

"Oh, no way!" she moaned. "Nothing good ever happens when you get that look on your face, Kaori." Nyaa-san batted her front paws against my leg in annoyance.

Sorry, Nyaa-san. There was just no way I could pass up an amazing opportunity like this.

Suimei was still thoroughly confused as I grabbed his arm. His eyes went wide, but I offered a bright smile. "All right, Suimei, why don't you come with me?" I said. "You know, I've been thinking about this for a while now, but I'm sure that if an exorcist actually had a chance to get to know all these spirits, they'd certainly get along. And it'll be a great experience to boot! So it's decided!"

"Whoa, wait a minute!" he protested. "I don't know where you got that crazy idea, but I'll never befriend a spirit!"

"Seeing is believing, you know? All right, Goblin-kun, take my hand. Now, let's go!" I cheerfully dragged them both along in my wake.

"Think of the people who will have to clean up after you for once," Nyaa-san said, sighing heavily, though the sound was quickly lost to the winds.

"Where are we?" Bewilderment and annoyance warred in Suimei's tone.

We'd headed down a long, dark alley to a dilapidated wooden door. I didn't bother answering Suimei before taking out a wet wipe to clean Goblin's hands. The poor guy looked like he wanted to cry when he realized the sugar stars he'd been clutching like precious treasures had melted in his hands.

"The stars, they melted..." he said.

"It's fine, I have more. Next time, I need to give you a wrapper to keep them in." I wiped away his tears and pinky promised that

I'd get more stars before the next time we met. He brightened instantly.

"You're always such a Goody Two-shoes, Kaori," Nyaa-san teased.

"Oh, be nice, Nyaa-san."

Suimei finally recovered enough from his confusion to interject. "Hey, aren't we off to meet the Yamajiji from Oboke? Oboke's in Tokushima Prefecture, you know. Are we going by plane? Train?"

"Huh? You mean public transportation? Out in the human world? No way, not a chance," I said. "Who knows when we'd even get there—and it's already too late at this point. Besides, I don't have that kind of money."

At this, he looked even more confused. "Then how do you plan to get there?"

"It's obvious, isn't it?" I smiled and turned the doorknob of the dilapidated door before us, only to be greeted by a clamorous roar and a warm blast of air.

Flames roared on the other side of the door. The moans of the dying whined under the snarls of angry demons and a raging fire. The glimmerflies surrounding me flapped away to escape the heat, though some were drawn to the red glow on the other side.

Suimei's face drained of color. "You can't be serious."

I couldn't suppress a grin. "Oh, I'm serious, all right."

He grabbed my arm. "What the literal hell are you talking about? No way!"

"All right, we're off!" I crowed. With that, I dove straight through the door, dragging the pale Suimei right along with me.

"Waaaaaaaaaugh!"

We began our rapid descent into said literal hell. Suimei's screams echoed throughout the chamber, briefly silencing the cries of the burning sinners. I reached out to Goblin as we continued to drop and searched for Nyaa-san. As I did, something large cushioned our fall.

"All right, Kaori, let's go," Nyaa-san said.

"Yep!"

That "something large" was Nyaa-san herself, now the size of a tiger. We sat on her back as she raced across glowing red magma. Up ahead, a figure stood atop the bridge linking the magma to the infernal lake of blood.

"Hey, Kaori, heading somewhere?" the figure called.

"As a matter of fact we are," I called back. "Oh, right, the fare... Here's a dumpling!"

"Ooh, nice! Thanks!"

"I bet it'd be even better if you roasted it in the fires over there. Anyway, see ya!"

"Have a safe trip!"

The red, horned oni dressed in little more than a loincloth waved happily before heading off to go roast his treat.

Nyaa-san bore us through a hollow in a large tree next to the infernal lake of blood. This teleported us to the human world. We emerged close to Oboke Gorge, located in the Yoshinogawa River Valley in Tokushima.

I hopped off Nyaa-san's back to survey our surroundings.

The sun had already set, and the cool night air chilled my skin.

The sudden temperature change left me covered in goosebumps. The only light came from a waning moon and the star-filled sky. Insects chirped in the foliage. We were far from civilization and therefore light pollution, which allowed us a stunning view of even the faintest stars.

"Wow..." I gaped at the twinkling human sky arrayed overhead. Though the spirit realm lived in a perpetual night, the beauty of this night was entirely its own.

Abruptly, someone grabbed my shoulder. I turned to find a very pale Suimei. "A-are you insane, riding through hell on top of a cat like that? How does that seem like a good idea to you?"

"Huh?" I blinked. "I mean, that's what it's always like when Shinonome-san and I go out."

The spirit realm wasn't merely the domain of spirits; it was also the land of the dead. Finding a door that led to the bowels of hell was hardly unusual. These doors connected to locations throughout Japan and didn't obey the laws of space-time, making them incredibly convenient for traveling just about anywhere.

Suimei dragged a hand through his white hair and mumbled under his breath. "Then you and that Shinonome guy are weirder than I thought, what with riding on a cat and all. And c'mon, you just tossed a dumpling to that oni like it was nothing? Are you friends? None of this makes any sense."

Was Suimei just tired from his ordeal? Where was this coming from? I pulled a water bottle out of my bag and passed it to him. He practically yanked it out of my hand and gulped down the contents. That seemed to help, at least. Maybe everything we'd just seen was a bit much for a normal human. I patted him on the back, feeling a bit guilty. He had just suffered that serious injury, after all.

"Well, you'll just have to get used to it, I guess," I said.

"I'll pass."

"Heh, when did you get back?" an unfamiliar voice said.

A blue-white ball of flame sprang to life from nowhere, rising into the air to bob around us. It quickly grew in intensity despite the lack of any fuel source and wove around as if it were trying to tease or maybe scare us away.

"An onibi? No, that's not right," I muttered.

An onibi occurred when a flame flared up with no apparent source or cause. Some blamed them on kitsune. But we were in Tokushima, which was more known for its tanuki spirits. In fact, we stood right on the location of the legend known as the Awa Tanuki Wars.

"So maybe it's a chochinbi?" I mused. Those were a kind of onibi associated with tanuki.

Just as the words left my mouth, a little tanuki leapt out of a nearby shrub. The thrill of guessing correctly faded as the spirit whirled and dashed off in the opposite direction, tail flopping as it bounded off.

Goblin took my hand and shouted with glee. "That's my friend! Hurry!"

"He's going to show us the way? Well, that's convenient."

Finding Yamajiji's ramshackle hut at night would have proved a real hassle, so I was glad to have a guide. Besides, there was something so quaint about walking along through the twilight as the tanuki's little butt swayed back and forth in front of us.

My mood lifted as we followed the little spirit. Then someone tugged on my arm, forcing us to stop. I glared over at Suimei.

"What's your problem?" I snapped.

"You've gotta be a real special kind of idiot to follow a tanuki into the mountains," he said. "That's gotta be something else in disguise."

Suimei's face still hadn't regained much color. I squinted after the tanuki, not yet convinced I needed to worry.

"What makes you so sure?" I asked. "And even if it *were* something in disguise, what's wrong with that? There's nothing to be scared of."

"Nnngh…" He clenched his fist, annoyance tightening his face.

Nyaa-san padded up and rubbed against my legs, fixing Suimei with a harsh look. "Kaori's always been like this, so the sooner you give up the better. Besides, as long as I'm here, there's nothing to worry about. You saw me back there, didn't you? Don't write me off as some ordinary house cat, okay?"

Suimei frowned. "Yeah, but…"

"Gah, you're a real stubborn one, aren't you?" Nyaa-san sighed. Then she grew right before our eyes, her bones creaking as they and her connective tissues expanded. In a matter of moments, the small black cat transformed into a massive, fanged beast. She snarled and snapped at Suimei. "You think I'm gonna let a little tanuki get the best of me?"

A deep crimson flame flickered out of Nyaa-san's mouth as she spoke. I sat back to enjoy the show. Nyaa-san and I had spent a long time together, after all, and I knew she was just messing with Suimei. If she were really angry, he wouldn't even be standing anymore.

It seemed her display did the trick. Suimei wiped the sweat from his brow and apologized.

A wagging tail led us along the animal trail through the forest.

Darkness closed in as we ventured even farther from human civilization. Thankfully, the tanuki's chochinbi, a sort of onibi, lit our way. Insects chirped at us as we disturbed the night, but we pushed on.

I turned to check on Suimei, but he was keeping up. He must have had some practice hiking. It made sense. Exorcists probably wound up chasing spirits up into the mountains all the time.

We continued like that for around fifteen minutes before the gurgle of flowing water broke the quiet.

"Yoshinogawa River! We're close!" Goblin cried.

He was right: We only had to trudge on for a few more minutes before we hit the Oboke Gorge. Starlight glistened off the river valley's metamorphic rock.

We hopped onto Nyaa-san's back so she could carry us into the valley below. The river lay dark right now, but I could imagine it gleaming in the sunlight, filled with tour boats and canoes.

Tonight, it contained only the watery reflection of the moon and a few pinpricks of light from the stars.

"It's right beyond that gash in the rock. Let's go!" Goblin urged.

"Watch your step," I said.

He yawned. "You know, I'm feeling pretty sleepy."

"Hey, don't leave me here!" Suimei yelled as we slid off Nyaa-san and headed for the gap Goblin had indicated.

"Hey, Yamajiji, you here?" I called.

We stepped through the gash and into a damp cave. Animal bones clattered beneath my feet, turning the floor treacherous. Water dripped somewhere in the distance, echoing in the dark cave. As we pushed deeper, a presence hung in the air, heavy and oppressive.

"What is it?" Suimei whispered.

"Shh!" I hissed. I grabbed Suimei to halt him and strained to see through the darkness ahead. Off in the inky blackness, just out of the range of the chochinbi's glow, I could make out something...or perhaps someone. "...Yamajiji?" I said, voice trembling.

Something lunged right at us.

"Watch out!" I cried.

"Aaah!" Suimei grabbed my hand and yanked me toward the wall and out of the way just as a loud crash clamored around us. I shivered as I peered down at the gash torn into the floor, as though someone had scooped out the stone like ice cream. I followed the gash and made out a humanoid silhouette ahead.

Crunch. Crunch. Ptooey.

The figure chewed on the stones it'd just scooped up before spitting them out. Ever so slowly, it turned to face us, finally exposing its features to the flickering light of the chochinbi.

The creature before us was...completely bizarre. It only stood about a hundred centimeters, but dark gray fur covered its entire body, like some fuzzy little animal. That only made its eyes creepier. They were off-kilter—one so small you might miss it and the other so large it took up most of its face.

Those strange, bloodshot eyes darted around before its lips stretched over its fangs in something like a smile.

"Oh...Yamajiji, it's been a while. I see you're doing well," Goblin said.

Nyaa-san responded first, growing in size again before diving at Yamajiji. I knew she was trying to keep me out of harm's way, but she put herself at risk in the process.

I called out to Suimei. "Hey, you're an exorcist, aren't you? Can't you do something about him?"

"Aah...oh, right!" Suimei dug in the pouch hanging from his waist and pulled out a glass bottle filled with some kind of hard, white substance. He grabbed the stopper but hesitated before actually pulling it out, and then he returned the bottle to his pouch with a sigh. "I can't freely use my abilities right now."

"Wait, what?"

"It's complicated."

"Right, great, I see." So much for that. I hunched down, rummaging through my backpack for my bag of medicine.

"You're not going to mock me for being so useless?" Suimei asked.

Huh? What was this all about? "Why would I do that?"

Though his face revealed as little as ever, I could tell he was deep in thought. I squinted, trying to puzzle out what he meant.

"Do you want me to talk down to you since you couldn't help?" I asked. "You're definitely a weird one. In that case, I should be mad at me too. Unlike the other beings in the spirit realm, I don't have any sort of special abilities to rely on."

"Really?" he said.

"Yep. As you can see, I'm just a normal human, but I still have a few tricks up my sleeve." I pressed the item I had pulled from my bag into Suimei's hand and smiled. "This'll solve all our problems. Now go for it."

"Hey, wait a second..."

We weren't going to get many shots at this. Nyaa-san had Yamajiji pinned down, so this was our best chance. I stepped cautiously forward.

"Stop jerking me around and tell me what's going on here!" Yamajiji howled.

"No one's jerking you around," Nyaa-san said.

I stepped up next to Yamajiji and pulled out a razor and a wet compress. "The compress will help for lower back pain, okay?"

While Nyaa-san held Yamajiji in place, I chopped away the fur on his lower back and pressed the wet compress to his exposed flesh.

"Uwaaaaaauuugh!" he wailed, his voice echoing through the chamber. He writhed, limbs lashing out, those strange eyes rolling. You see, that compress was a special one just for spirits. Whatever it was doing, it was quite effective.

I searched for Suimei, who looked even paler than when we'd jumped into hell. "Hurry up and put it on!" I urged. "Can't you see he's in pain?"

"Aren't you the one who hurt him?" he said. He dabbed at his head like he was trying to fight off a headache.

"I didn't hurt him at all!"

"Wait, so...he's thrashing around like that because his back hurts?" Suimei said.

"That's right. He throws his back out like this sometimes. Unlike humans, who are usually able to cope with injuries like that, spirits tend to go a little wild. It's kinda weird, I know."

While we spoke, I slapped the other compress on, resulting in a whimper from Yamajiji before he began to convulse. The poor spirit was still clearly in pain. I'd need to spread this out a bit.

"Hey, I'm really sorry about this, Yamajiji, but I'm going to have to shave away some more fur," I said. "Just hang in there, okay?"

"Nooo...ngyaaaaaaaaa!" he groaned.

I shaved away patches of fur at random and slapped on more compresses, each application resulting in another cry and more convulsions. Soon, compresses almost entirely covered Yamajiji's lower back, but he was finally returning to normal.

I breathed out a sigh of relief. "Wow, that was pretty crazy."

Yamajiji gingerly sat up, glaring in my direction. Nevertheless, his pain must have eased, because his eyes weren't nearly so bloodshot and he could evidently think clearly again. He sniffed at the compresses on his back while I poured him a glass of alcohol.

"I'm glad you're back to normal," I said.

"The back pain was bad, for sure, but having you slap those down on me like that was pretty awful," Yamajiji mumbled. He noisily sucked down the drink I offered, then gaped at the empty cup.

"Huh?" I frowned. "But Shinonome-san said to always slap on the compresses as hard as you can."

"Mind if I take a bite out of your old man for that?" he snorted. "Just a nibble."

"Not at all, he's all yours."

Yamajiji's bite strength was so powerful that he could probably crush the head of a wild boar. I didn't think Shinonome-san would let himself get gnawed on so easily, but it would be fun to at least watch the old man have to run around to escape Yamajiji's ire. I giggled at the mental image as I refilled Yamajiji's cup.

Suimei watched on silently. He didn't look the least bit relaxed, still eyeing Yamajiji warily.

"Come on over, Suimei," I said. "It's okay now."

"No thanks."

I smiled wryly at his stubbornness. I supposed it only made sense that someone who made a living by exorcising spirits wouldn't trust them so easily.

Yamajiji downed his second cup in a single gulp. "Hey, what brings you here anyway?" he asked. "You didn't come all the way out here just to fix my back, did you?"

"Oh, that's right!" I clapped my hands. "Goblin-kun wanted you to read him a book."

"Huh?"

Yamajiji and I searched for Goblin and found him shyly peeking out from behind a rock.

"Heyyy, Goblin-kuuun," I called.

"Eek!" he squeaked.

Despite my efforts to wave him over, Goblin only stood there trembling, hugging his tanuki companion close to his chest. It seemed he'd never seen Yamajiji really lose it like that. In general, Yamajiji were benign, so the sudden change must have been quite alarming.

Nyaa-san wasn't taking "no" for an answer, though. She hefted Goblin up by the scruff of his neck and carried him over. "Stop playing games and get out here."

Nyaa-san dumped Goblin unceremoniously in front of Yamajiji. Goblin shuddered and shook, clutching his tanuki, who now scrambled to escape. Yamajiji reached out and affectionately mussed the trembling kid's hair.

"So, you wanted me to read you a book, huh?" he said.

"Uh...um. A-are you okay now?" Goblin asked. "You're back to normal? You're not gonna gobble me up, right, Yamajiji?"

"Of course not! Now gimme that book." Yamajiji took the book in his oversized hands and squinted. "It's way too dark to read over here, but I've got a nice place a little deeper in. Follow me."

Yamajiji took Goblin's hand and led him deeper into the cave, to a place where a hole in the ceiling allowed the light of the moon to filter in. Compared to the rest of the cave, it almost looked like a stage illuminated by a spotlight. Yamajiji and Goblin settled down with the book, Goblin's fears apparently allayed.

"Long, long ago," Yamajiji read.

The Yamajiji were known for their loud voices. According to some, they could cause all sorts of natural disasters just by belting one out. Though this Yamajiji was certainly quite loud, his voice didn't strike me as all that menacing as he read. In fact, there was something quite soothing about the way his words reverberated through the rocky cave. A light scratchiness added age to the smooth notes of his voice.

"The round, yellow moon..." he went on.

I closed my eyes and sank into the story. His unique Awa accent made his voice rich, like syrup pouring into my ears and spreading warmth through my whole body.

Before I knew it, Suimei sat next to me, watching the spirits in front of us.

"Thanks," I whispered, hoping not to interrupt the reading.

"What for?" he asked, eyes narrowing in suspicion.

"The compress. I appreciated your help."

"I don't recall doing anything particularly helpful..."

"Hm, well you were at least there with me."

"Last I checked, you dragged me after you."

Suimei's scowl deepened as we spoke. He seemed determined to disagree no matter what I said. I chuckled and shook my head. What a weird guy. It had to be tough living life that way, being so stubborn and set in your ways. Well, at least he was straightforward.

"You're an interesting one, you know that?" I said.

"Where'd that come from all of a sudden?" Suimei snorted and turned his head away. I couldn't help but chuckle in spite of myself. He was way too easy to tease.

"I'm glad Goblin-kun got to read his book," I said, focusing on the storytelling instead.

Suimei remained silent and stared straight ahead.

"You know, you seem to be in a pretty bad mood. What's wrong?" I asked.

"Bad mood? Me? No way."

"Well, you certainly don't seem to be in a good mood."

Suimei's shoulders slumped as he watched the two figures reading under the light of the moon. "I'm an exorcist," he said eventually. "In fact, I'm the heir to a long line of exorcists. My body may be battered and beaten right now, but up until a short time ago, I'd taken on my fair share of jobs and exorcised a bunch of spirits."

"Huh, who'd have thunk it?"

"Has anyone ever told you that you never know when to just stay quiet?" Suimei sighed. "Anyway, like I said, I'm an exorcist. And exorcists need spirits to make a living. Spirits exist to be exorcised. They should be loathed and exterminated by humans. ...That's what I was taught and believed. But was it all true? Here they are, just focused on reading a book, even while humans are so close by. How can you hate that? They're completely absorbed in the story. A story written by humans, no less. I just...don't know what to think."

Suimei averted his eyes, lost in his own thoughts. I examined him, inspecting his face, searching for something in that blank void. Then I poked his cheek with a finger.

"Eh, what now?" he muttered.

"Your cheeks are so soft," I observed. "If only you'd let the rest of your face soften up like that too."

I grinned as I pinched both of his cheeks, tugging at the pliable flesh. Suimei struggled to pull away, but I refused to let go.

"They live in the same country, share the same language, and even live in the same age as we do," I said. "Why would you think they *wouldn't* love the same stories as we do?"

Suimei stopped struggling and went quiet. I continued to prod his cheeks as I spoke.

"I mean, granted, humans and spirits have different moral persuasions, to say nothing of their bodies, appearances, and upbringings. But we all live in the same place, don't we? We all see the same things. So of course these stories appeal to all of us. These fanciful tales written by humans contain the power to entice people and spirits just the same."

I let go of his cheeks to gaze into his brown eyes.

"Sure, there are some spirits out there who attack humans," I said. "That's why we need the power of the exorcists. But I don't want you to lump all spirits together in the same category. There are also plenty of spirits like these here. In fact, I hope that someday, humans and spirits can come together and learn to be friends."

Suimei just shook his head. "That seems...unlikely. Most

humans don't even take kindly to other humans different from themselves."

"You're right there," I admitted.

I didn't harbor any fantastical dreams of a world where spirits and humans lived together in perfect harmony. All I really hoped for was peace and friendship inside my little bubble. Alas, even that seemed like a pipe dream at the moment.

"It just wouldn't really work out, huh?" I sighed.

"Pretty much..." Suimei said.

I sighed again and focused on Goblin and Yamajiji to banish my bleak thoughts.

The bright moonlight shining through the roof enveloped them in a soft glow. Now that I looked a little closer, I noticed that other spirits had joined us, though many seemed to be tanuki, thanks to the location. Everyone stood completely still as they listened intently to Yamajiji. For this moment, at least, the rift between the humans who'd written the story and the spirits reading it evaporated in the simple pleasure of enjoying the tale.

"Hey, Kaori," Suimei said.

"Yes?"

He spoke slowly, chewing over each word. "What are you? Human? Spirit?"

I responded without a moment's hesitation. After all, I'd spent years wondering the same myself. "Just going by my body alone, definitely human. But my heart... I think my heart might be with spirits. Or humans? I really don't know. It's kinda strange, isn't it? It's like I exist in some kind of middle ground, belonging to neither one side nor the other."

It almost felt like an introduction. Though, now that I thought about it, I'd never actually properly introduced myself to Suimei. I wiped my hand off on my clothes and extended it to him.

"I'm Muramoto Kaori," I said. "I realize I can come off as a bit impulsive sometimes, but I'm pleased to meet you all the same."

Suimei showed only a moment's hesitation before gripping my hand in his own. "Pleased to meet you. I'm Shirai Suimei. I may be clumsy, but I'm an exorcist who prides himself on being able to see through spirits' tricks. Or should I say, an ex-exorcist... My family's closed up shop." I wanted to tease him, but he looked a bit torn up about it. It was just so hard to keep from trading verbal barbs with him, even in a situation like this.

I reclined against the cool rock wall to continue listening to Yamajiji. As he read, the hero of the story tripped over a rock and tumbled head over heels, landing right in a pile of manure. Everyone listening broke out in a fit of laughter, myself included. Suimei, however, simply looked perplexed.

I closed my eyes, drifting into a contented half-doze. The peace afforded by sharing this story wrapped around me like a warm blanket.

"Why you impertinent little...! Did you ever bother to think about how a parent would feel coming home to find their daughter and an injured boy missing?!"

"I...I'm sorry."

Suimei and I sat side by side across from Shinonome-san, whose face burned red with anger. He puffed away at his pipe and tapped his foot incessantly, as though the irritation simply couldn't be contained in his body. Meanwhile, Suimei and I had our heads bowed and our legs folded neatly under us. Nyaa-san, realizing that things were going to get ugly, quietly slipped upstairs. Traitor.

"Goblin-kun came here in tears saying that Yamajiji from Oboke threw out his back again," I said. "But I'm sorry I didn't think to leave a note for you. I'll be sure to do that next time."

My adoptive father's face tightened. Still, after only another moment of glaring, the rage gave way to weary acceptance. "Yamajiji, huh? Poor guy. Well, I guess it is what it is."

I giggled and threw my arms around him. "Aww, you're a real softie. I knew you couldn't stay mad."

"Hey, no hugs! You're so hot—and heavy too!"

"Whoa, heavy? You didn't need to go there!"

"So, um, about me..." Suimei spoke up.

"What about you?" asked Shinonome-san. "You're still here, huh? Well, you look fine, so you ought to be getting home."

After checking that Suimei's bleeding had stopped, Shinonome-san gestured toward the exit with his chin. Suimei looked pleadingly at me before turning back to Shinonome-san and bowing his head.

"I know it's rather sudden, but could I stay here for a while longer?" he asked.

"Wha?" Shinonome-san blinked.

"There's something I need to do here," Suimei said. "Would you please consider it?"

Shinonome-san scowled at the sudden request. He leaned in close to Suimei, staring straight into his eyes. Then he snorted with laughter. "Unfortunately for you, kid, your chest is flatter than a washing board, and you've got a butt to go along with it. So I'm gonna have to say...no!"

Suimei and I were both completely taken aback by this response.

"Is that really how you make your decisions?" Suimei muttered.

I gasped. "Whoa, wait a sec, so you're saying he'd be in if he had a huge rack or a big butt?"

Shinonome-san backed up ever so slightly. "No, no...that was a joke, you see. A joke! Ah ha ha ha!"

Shinonome-san attempted to backpedal, but I wasn't about to let him talk his way out of this one. I crossed my arms and fixed Shinonome-san with a steely glare as sweat beaded on his forehead.

"You're awful," I said.

"No, you've got it all wrong!" he protested. "It was a joke! Okay, so I shouldn't make such off-color jokes in front of my daughter, but—hey, you, you're a man. Back me up here!"

"I mean, I really don't know what to say..." Suimei said.

Knowing it was a joke did nothing to ease the bad taste in my mouth. I half closed my eyes and sniffed as I stepped behind Suimei. Shinonome-san slumped. Suimei just pulled out his wallet and tossed something on the tatami flooring.

Shinonome-san and I froze at the sight.

"Listen, I'm not asking you to let me just laze about your house," Suimei said. "I have no intention of staying here for free."

Fukuzawa Yukichi's face looked blankly back up at us—the man drawn on the ten-thousand-yen bill. And he wasn't alone. He sat atop a whole stack of identical ones.

Suimei pushed the stack of money toward Shinonome-san.

"I'm looking for a particular spirit," he said, "so it'd be easier for me if I could just work from here. I know that humans stand out, but I figure with Kaori also living in the same house, well... Hey, are you listening?"

"Shinonome-san..." I said.

"What, Kaori?"

Shinonome-san and I gawked at the bills. I couldn't have opened my eyes any wider even if I tried. Suimei observed us placidly.

"Are these real?" Shinonome-san murmured.

"Maybe they're some kind of play money?" I murmured back.

"Huh, that'd make sense. Just for play, I guess."

Our excitement ramped up as we inspected the bills. The closer we looked, the more it became apparent that these were real. I glanced back at Suimei and broke out into a fit of laughter. "These are pretty good fakes!"

"What's with you guys?" Suimei asked, frowning. "You're pretty eager to just write these off as counterfeits."

He seemed so insistent that this wasn't some sort of joke, but that couldn't possibly be. Were these really, really *real*?

I jerked my head back up and grabbed both of Suimei's hands in my own. "You mean that you'll give this to us if we let you stay here?"

"I, uh, of course," he said. "I mean, your expenses and everything are going to increase with another person living with you, right?"

"That's right, of course they are! It'll be a real hassle, ya know, having another person around."

Suimei offered a quick nod. "In that case, I'll pay the same amount every month. You can think of it as rent."

"Every month?" I gaped.

"Um, correct."

Shinonome-san shouted as he finished counting the bills. "Hey, Kaori! There's two hundred thousand here! I can't believe it, two hundred thousand!"

I swallowed hard and looked Suimei right in the eyes. "Are you sure about this?"

"It's fine by me," he insisted.

My whole body shook as I faced Shinonome-san. He wore a broad grin as he gave me the thumbs up. I nodded and turned back toward Suimei, a newfound excitement fluttering in my chest.

"Welcome to the haunted bookstore!" I declared. "It's old, run-down, and a bit cramped, but please make yourself at home."

"Hey, no need to talk down about a man's castle, you know!" Shinonome-san protested.

"I mean, it's true. Try opening your eyes for once, old man," I sniffed.

"Why I—I don't even know what to say to you." Shinonome-san jabbed a finger at me. "This has nothing to do with the state of the house. Anyway, let's put that aside. I want meat! Go buy the best, highest-quality meat you can find. Something with some nice, delicious fat that'll melt away under the slightest touch."

"Whoa, hang on! We need to watch our spending, you know. But I guess we can do it just this once and send one of these bills off to a new home. I'll be back." I leapt up, waving as I threw open the sliding door connecting home and shop, and slipped on some sandals.

"Hey, wait!" Suimei called.

I paused at his desperate tone. Face taut, Suimei reached out to me as though seeking help. "Don't leave me here alone with the old man."

Shinonome-san laughed. "What're you talking about? We're gonna be sharing everything from now on, aren't we? Let's sit around and talk, like men."

The scowl on Suimei's face spoke louder than any words he could have chosen then. "No way, quit it. Stay away from me. I'm totally out."

"Hey, don't be shy. Back me up, Kaori!" Shinonome-san commanded.

I shook my head, chuckling at the playful exchange, and made my escape. The moment I stepped outside, glimmerflies descended around me, illuminating the spirit world as they batted about my shoulders.

I didn't get far before a harried voice cried out to me.

"Hang in there until I get back, Suimei!" I called back. "Don't let the old man get the best of you."

"You can't be serious!" he cried.

"See you!"

With that, I skipped away into the town of eternal darkness.

CHAPTER 2

The Giant Fuji Spirit

EVEN IN THE EARLY MORNING, darkness cloaked the spirit realm.

The stars glimmered spectacularly—even brighter than they did at night—their many hues blending into a fuzzy halo. Shattered emerald fragments twinkled in the sky. Even in the thick of rainy season, a refreshing breeze dried the laundry hanging on the line outside on a clear, crisp day.

I leaned out my window to soak in the sky. Ittan-momen, a spirit made of rolls of cotton, waved as he wafted by. It was going to be a beautiful day, I just knew it, so I decided to air out my futon while I stretched my back.

Morning was the busiest part of my day. Without a mother around, all the housekeeping fell to me or it didn't get done at all. Laundry, breakfast, cleaning...day in and day out, the chores stacked up.

"Where's breakfast, Kaori?" Shinonome-san called.

"Yeah, yeah, I know," I said.

"Hey, make mine first, and not the one in the can. I hate that," Nyaa-san said.

"I hear you!"

The stairs creaked while I prepared rice and miso soup. Shinonome-san hardly ever woke up on his own, so I figured the one coming down had to be Suimei. I confirmed my suspicion with a look over my shoulder. Suimei was wearing one of the old man's yukata and rubbing the drowsiness from his eyes, looking even younger than usual in his oversized borrowed clothing.

"Morning, Suimei."

"Hm, good mo...ah!"

"What is it?" I asked.

Suimei froze in place. Maybe he was feeling sick?

"Do any of your injuries hurt?" I asked as I hurried over to him. I worried that he might have pushed himself too far so soon after recovering. "You're probably still tired. Maybe you should rest some more."

"N-no. Th-that's not it." Suimei trembled and took several steps away from me as though trying to escape. He seemed confused, even a bit shaken. After a moment, I recognized the look.

"It's still dark here in the morning, so it doesn't really feel like you woke up, huh?" I smiled. "I lived up in the human world for a while when I was attending high school, and I have to say that it was extremely unsettling when I came back here."

"I don't think I'll ever get used to the morning being so dark..." he muttered. "But more importantly, you graduated high school?"

"Of course, and a while ago at that. I'm twenty, you know."

"No way." Suimei pinched the bridge of his nose. "You know, I kind of figured we were the same age."

"Huh?" It was obvious that *he* was still a high school student... but us, the same age? I slapped my hands to my face to cover the flush rising in my cheeks. I didn't really think of myself as old, but I was still happy to be mistaken for someone in their teens. "How old are *you*, Suimei?"

"Seventeen," he admitted. "Anyway, don't get ahead of yourself. I was just surprised that someone like you could actually be older than me."

"Someone like me—what's that supposed to mean?" I pouted, narrowing my eyes.

He took off the haori he was wearing over his yukata and tossed it at me. "Let me make one thing clear. I'm not your family. I may be younger than you, but I'm still a man, and don't you forget it. So try to conduct yourself like someone your age ought to, got it?"

"Huh? What're you..."

"I'm going to wash my face." He stalked off without another word, but a flush brightened his neck and ears.

Just what had that been about? I held out the haori he'd handed me and glanced down at myself. Suddenly, it all made sense. "Eep!"

It had been hot and humid the night before, so I'd slept in a tank top and hot pants with a thin jumper thrown on over the top. I hugged the haori close and yelled back toward Suimei: "Sorry about that!"

"Whatever, just change!" he shouted back.

I couldn't help but laugh at the annoyance in his voice.

After changing, I went to find Shinonome-san and discovered him still sleeping, his covers bunched up in his arms like a large body pillow.

"All right, get up." I ripped the covers out of his grasp and started cleaning up the manuscript papers scattered all over the floor. He merely rolled over.

Then, suddenly: "Waaaaaaugh!"

"S-Suimei?!" I gasped. I recognized that yelp.

"Augh!" Shinonome-san groaned as I stepped right on him in my haste to scramble to the well in the backyard.

I bolted through the living room, then threw open the sliding door leading to the backyard and slipped on some sandals. Off in one corner of the moss-covered yard sat a small well that we used for most of our washing up in the morning. That had to be the source of the disturbance, but surprise prevented me from getting any closer.

"Wh-who are you?! What're you doing in Kaori's yard?" Suimei demanded.

A massive raven was attacking him, pecking at his head and sending feathers flying through the yard.

"Oh, hey, Kaori. Just stopping by," said a boy suddenly.

I'd completely missed him until he spoke. He sat in a corner, looking like a raven himself with his hair dark as silky black wings and his sleepy golden eyes. He held a red ceremonial staff, and a hood shaded his face. All in all, it made him look like some sort of monk or other practitioner. Though he seemed like a normal human, the four black, glowing talons at his feet gave him away as a bird spirit.

I smiled and waved. "Oh, hi, Kinme. Hey, is that Ginme over there?"

"Yup. He wanted to come see you, so we rushed through our morning training and came on over only to find this suspicious guy out here. He kinda lost it after that."

"Hmm, you don't say."

Kinme was the twin brother of the bird currently attacking Suimei. In contrast to Kinme's calm, easy demeanor, Ginme tended to act first and ask questions later. It caused no shortage of trouble. I'd known both of them since I was only five. At the time, they'd been injured little fledglings rejected by their parents. I'd done what I could to help, and we'd been close ever since. I was a bit tighter with Ginme, who'd often come to the house to hang out with me when we were kids. I'd always seen him as a sort of little brother, but he looked at things differently. What a pain.

I put my hands on my hips and yelled. "Cut it out! I'm gonna get real angry if you don't settle down!"

"Huh?!" Ginme abruptly backed off of Suimei and transformed into his human form in midair. Unsurprisingly, he looked just like his twin, except for his silver pupils, cheery eyes, and the blue staff he carried. Ginme recovered himself and grinned as he approached. "G'morning, Kaori! How're you?"

"I'm good. I see you're chipper today."

"Yep, always am."

I couldn't help imagining a dog's tail wagging behind Ginme as he spoke. Suimei, however, had blood trickling down his head. Wariness and weariness warred on his face.

"So who's that?" Ginme asked.

"That's Suimei," I explained. "He started living with us as of yesterday."

"Living with you?!"

Ginme bristled, but Kinme just crossed his arms. "So, is this the human who they said came tumbling down to the street?" he asked.

"You know about that?" I shrugged. "Well, I guess spirits do love to gossip. Anyway, he's searching for some spirit or another and wanted to use our house as a base of operations, so we let him stay here."

"Shinonome was okay with that?" Kinme frowned.

"Of course."

"Whoa...really?" Ginme held his head in his hands, muttering under his breath about me and Suimei being under the same roof together. I kept my face carefully blank and ignored his distress as I approached Suimei.

Blood soaked the bandages around Suimei's head, while small cuts marred his face. He looked pretty well worked over. "Are you okay?" I asked. "I'm really sorry about Ginme. It looks like your old wounds opened back up, so we'll need to get you some more medicine."

"It's nothing, just a couple of scratches," he muttered.

"No way. It could start to fester if you leave it alone." I reached out to try to check on his wounds, but he batted my hand away.

"Cut it out." There was an uneasy look in his hazel eyes, almost as if he wasn't used to being touched.

I mumbled an apology. "I'm going to head out after breakfast, okay?"

"Well, if you're going to the pharmacy or whatever, that's fine by me." Suimei sighed. "I'm not too fussed about getting injured. I'm an outsider, after all, so I kind of expected it."

It was nice to hear he wasn't too bothered, though I suspected he'd hold a grudge against Ginme after all this. He narrowed his eyes and shot Ginme a look. "But I have to say, that bird over there is incredibly rude," Suimei said. "He hasn't offered an apology, even after learning that I'm your guest. If he thinks you can just apologize *for* him and that'll be it, then it doesn't seem we'll see eye to eye anytime soon."

"What?!" Ginme stepped toward Suimei, looming. He stood at least two heads taller than Suimei, but the young exorcist didn't back down. I braced for another fight, but just when it looked like it might break out, Ginme gave in. "I guess you're right," he said. "So we'll be good if I just apologize, then?"

"Pretty much," Suimei confirmed.

"Gotcha. Well, sorry."

"We're good, then." Suimei nodded curtly and made his way back to the house. The matter was settled as far as he was concerned.

Ginme blinked at Suimei's retreating back before letting out a cheerful laugh. "You're one funny guy!" He rushed up behind Suimei and grabbed him by the shoulder. "I think we should be friends. Suimei, was it? I'm Ginme."

"Shut up." Suimei brushed him off. "I have no intention of being friends with the likes of you."

"Heh, you even sound cool! I mean, you're a tiny little runt, but you're cool!"

"You could have shut your mouth halfway through that, you know."

"Hey, don't be so cold," Kinme joined in. "Anyway, listen, I'm sorry about my brother. I'm Kinme, but you can call me Kin-chan."

"A nickname?" Suimei snorted. "Idiot. Didn't I just say that I had no intention of befriending you?"

"Aw, c'mon, that again?" Kinme chuckled. "Listen, it's not like you have anything to lose." He set his hand on Suimei's other shoulder that Ginme hadn't claimed.

Suimei sank under the strength of the two tall spirits. "Cut it out. You guys are heavy…"

Kinme grinned. "Ah, sorry about that. You're a tiny wee thing. I didn't even think about it."

"No, you're just big. Gah." Suimei batted away the brothers' hands.

"I guess boys make friends pretty easily, huh…?" I mused. I chuckled at the thought, knowing I had nothing more to worry about, at least not between those three. "Well, let's eat!"

"Huh, us too?" Kinme perked up.

"If you haven't already eaten, that is," I said.

"I ate, but I can definitely eat again!" Ginme declared.

"I don't get you…" Suimei sighed.

Breakfast was definitely going to be lively this particular morning. I waved everyone into the house before heading to the kitchen to start preparing the meal.

"Heh, the twins are here?" Shinonome-san asked.

"Hiya!" The twins cheerfully greeted a groggy Shinonome-san before slipping into the role of my kitchen helpers. Today's breakfast was going to be eggs served sunny-side up with bacon. On the side, I added some cherry tomatoes, miso soup with wheat gluten cake, glistening white rice, and natto with pollock roe.

Everyone crowded around the table as white wisps of steam curled up from the neatly arrayed food. Everyone except Suimei, who stood alone in the corner looking distinctly uncomfortable with the whole affair.

"What's wrong?" I asked him. "Let's eat."

"Ah, sorry." Suimei hesitantly sat down on the pillow that marked his place at the table. He definitely seemed off, but everyone else put their hands together and blessed the meal. Except, again, for Suimei. He stood apart, muttering under his breath after the rest of us said our blessing.

Suimei might have been holding back, but Ginme certainly wasn't. He dove for his chopsticks with a grin. "Man, I'm starving!"

"Didn't you already eat?" Kinme said.

"I've already digested all that." Ginme shoveled rice into his mouth with glee. He emptied his bowl in record time and stared down at it with curiosity. "Mmm, what is this? It's amazing!"

Kinme also looked quite surprised when he tried his dish. "Did you use a different rice?"

I could hardly contain my satisfaction. "This is actually a special A-grade rice, I'll have you know. I picked it up when I went out to buy some meat yesterday."

"Whooooa!"

I earned several gasps of amazement with this revelation. A-grade was the highest quality of rice. I'd picked it up on a whim after remembering Suimei's remark about how mediocre our rice was. Apparently, I'd chosen a winner. Even Shinonome-san, who usually didn't finish his meal, was quietly munching away.

Time to try it myself. I scooped up some rice, holding it in my mouth. Tears sprang to the corners of my eyes as the flavor hit me. I could feel each and every grain, soft but resistant. And that sweetness! It spread through my mouth with each bite, leaving me stunned as I absorbed the deliciously gentle flavor. Thank goodness I'd been born Japanese. No budget rice blend could ever compare to what I was experiencing right at that instant.

"Mmm...pure bliss. I guess this is all thanks to you, Suimei. So, thanks!" I beamed in his direction, only to find him staring blankly down at his bowl.

Oh, no. Was he not feeling well? Worry nagged at my mind, but after a moment, he finally started eating. "Hmph, it's all right."

Sitting next to Suimei, Ginme's eyes nearly popped out of his head. "You can't be serious! Just what kind of glamorous food are you used to? Try some of these pickled vegetables. The young lady next door's been making these at home ever since she got married about two hundred years ago, and they're absolutely to die for."

"Two hundred years?" Suimei furrowed his brow as he inspected the pickle. "Two hundred years, but you still consider her a young lady?"

"Well, I mean, she is," Ginme said.

Suimei muttered something to himself. Seriously, what was that all about?

At least his banter with Ginme had eased the mood, though something still seemed off to me. Thankfully, my rice was an excellent distraction. Soon enough, I had to go to the kitchen to fetch seconds for everyone.

Strictly speaking, there were no doctors in the spirit realm.

The majority of spirits chose to heal their own wounds, no matter how severe. Yamajiji, whom we'd dealt with just the other day, was no different. Even if it meant practically losing their mind with pain, very few spirits would go see a doctor for help. Maybe that sort of thing was more of a human concept. Spirits seemed to regard it as strange. They kind of resembled animals in that respect.

However, off in a corner of town, we did have an apothecary. My town was the largest and most prosperous in all the spirit realm. That brought with it a lot of movement back and forth with the human world, as well as a certain amount of familiarity with human customs and values. Still, exposure to the human world carried the risk of running into exorcists, hence the need for some sort of medical institution to help injured spirits. That was where the apothecary came in, prescribing medicine and performing basic medical procedures for the spirits in town.

And that's right where I was headed. As I rounded the corner of the shop, the atmosphere changed completely. A riot of smells hit my nose: a whiff of dead grass, something sweet, something sour, and something else powerful yet unnameable. The various medicinal herbs the apothecary kept on hand produced the potent perfume that marked our destination.

Even the building stood out. Outside, we saw a decorative wooden board of Chinese aesthetic, inscribed with a variety of intricate characters and symbols. The meticulous carving showed age, but it had withstood the test of time. Inside, shelves overflowing with glass bottles surrounded a desk with a mortar and pestle sitting atop it. Then, of course, there was the shop's owner.

"Welcome, welcome," the owner said. Her lovely lips curved as she glanced over my shoulder. Long lashes framed her richly amber eyes. There was something enchanting about the depth of their color.

Suimei tensed up under her gaze.

The owner's smile curled into a coquettish smirk. As she ran a hand through her moss green hair, the color shifted and glowed. To top it all off, a pair of bull horns crested her head, which was ever so slightly smaller than the average human's. "I'm guessing you want more of your usual ointment?" she said.

Before I even had a chance to say anything, the apothecary started rummaging through the shelves. I thanked her, and she winked in return.

The apothecary's name was...well, she didn't actually have a name. In fact, since she was always telling people that she had no name, the spirits around town had taken to calling her Noname. Shinonome-san and Noname went way back, though there was something about her appearance that made her look distinctly not Japanese. As for what a non-Japanese spirit would be doing running a business in an otherwise Japanese spirit realm, I couldn't really say.

Despite her mysterious origins, Noname had looked after me ever since I was young, even though I wasn't a spirit. She had even provided me with incense that drove the glimmerflies away from our home at the bookstore. If Shinonome-san was like my father, then Noname was like my mother.

"All right, just wait a moment," she said. "Ginme, don't you dare touch the shelves."

"I know, I know..." he said.

"Keep an eye on your brother, Kinme. No pranks, got it?"

Noname gathered ingredients while we browsed the shop. It was full of so many rare and interesting things that I never got bored. Sure, some of the bottles—the ones filled with eyeballs and the like—were kind of disgusting, but my opinion of them softened when I considered how they were used to treat injuries.

Strangely enough, Suimei seemed quite familiar with many of the herbs and other ingredients on display. I supposed that was necessary if you worked as an exorcist. He perused the shop with great interest, eyes widening when he picked out some item that was especially hard to get in the human world.

Suddenly Ginme's face lit up. He held a bottle full of candy aloft and looked toward Noname, but paused before calling out for her, cocking his head to the side. "Hey, is that a lady or a man?"

A vein bulged in Noname's forehead.

Uh-oh.

Kinme, blissfully oblivious to Noname's ire, smirked at Ginme before responding. "According to Noname, she's an uncle with the heart of a young maiden. So I guess you just call 'er whatever you want."

"Huh. Hey, Uncle—" Ginme said.

Two hands adorned with poison-green nail polish launched out and grabbed the bird twins by their heads. Noname let out a sinister cackle. "Shut your mouths, my little magpies..."

"Owww, your nails are digging into my skin!" Kinme yelped.

"Hey, we're no magpies! We're raven Tengu, I'll have you know!" Ginme wailed.

"And yet your brains are as tiny as your smallest cousins'!" Noname said. "Hmph... Anyway, what are these scratches on you? Did you get into a fight or something? You'd best rub on this ointment."

Noname held the boys in place with a powerful arm while using her free hand to retrieve a bottle from the shelf. They went pale, struggling in her grasp.

"Wait, not the mustard!" Ginme cried.

"Nooo! That one hurts and always makes me cry!" Kinme sobbed.

"You know, lady, I think your eyes have been going bad lately. You can't see we're right as rain!"

They both glared at Noname and did their best to wriggle away.

"What are you talking about—all three of my eyes are just fine!" Noname cackled as the third eye on her forehead opened and began to glow. With an expert hand, she applied the mustard directly to the raven twins' wounds—the ones she'd inflicted—eliciting high-pitched screams. Suimei and I threw our hands over our ears.

She wasn't done yet, however. Suimei was her next victim. He endured a pearl-colored ointment that made him wince every time Noname applied it to a cut. She just smiled, holding him in place.

"You're fine," she said. "This may be medicine meant for spirits, but it'll work just as well on humans. Look at her if you don't believe me."

"I've used it often," I agreed. "Before I know it, the cuts have healed up perfectly without a mark."

"That's right." Noname nodded. "I'll have you know that this runt was always getting herself hurt when she was little. She'd get herself all roughed up and then come rolling on in here begging me to fix her up. Shinonome-san would always go on about how he'd have my head if I left a scar on his little girl. I'm telling you, it was a real hassle."

I grinned. "Hey, at least it's not so often now."

"Lies. Remember the end of last year when you scraped your kneecap?"

"I couldn't see where I was going!"

Noname only smirked at my protests. The excuse meant nothing to her.

Okay, fine. Maybe I had been so focused on that meat kabob that I'd completely missed the Sunekosuri. But still!

A Sunekosuri, by the way, was a spirit from Okayama Prefecture known for scraping people's legs and making it difficult to walk. It was fluffy and pure white, and it looked like either a dog or a cat. It was actually quite cute when you watched it waddling around, but the moment it made contact with a leg, it could make even the biggest spirit cringe in terror. Most of the denizens of the spirit realm avoided Sunekosuri without even really thinking about it.

Noname chuckled as I finally mumbled to concede her point. Then her expression went soft. Too soft, in fact.

"You've really never grown up, you know," she said. "You'd best hurry up and find yourself a nice family to marry into and stop relying on me."

"Oh, c'mon, not you too?" I moaned. Gah, that again. I pouted, exhausted with this tired subject. "Maybe when Shinonome-san can take care of himself."

"Well, that'll never happen. Not that dimwit!" Noname sniffed.

As we bantered, Noname redid Suimei's bandages. She patted his arm when she was finished. "All done."

"Hmph...thanks," he grumbled.

"It's nothing."

Suimei scowled and winced while Noname inspected him.

"You're pretty frank, kid," she said. "That's a good thing. Not only are you unafraid of spirits you know nothing about, you even properly thanked me. Not many humans could do that." Noname batted away some of the glimmerflies clustered around Suimei, weighing him in her amber gaze. He tensed under the scrutiny. "I heard you nigh instantly forgave the magpies even after they attacked you. That's *quite* impressive. I wonder if all humans are like that now. Or is it because you're an exorcist that you see no reason to worry about little birds like them?"

Suimei dove suddenly backward, smashing into one of the shelves and sending bottles crashing to the floor. He crouched like a cornered beast and glared forward, his eyes wide and un-blinking. The whole movement took me completely by surprise. How could a friendly conversation turn so abruptly into a fight?!

"Kaori..." Suimei growled as he turned his glare on me.

"I didn't say anything! Really, I didn't!" I protested. But I couldn't really blame him. Shinonome-san and I both under-stood that we had to keep Suimei's profession under wraps here in the spirit realm or he'd be in a heap of trouble.

Noname stepped slowly toward Suimei. "Kaori said nothing to me."

Suimei's eyes darted as he sized up the encroaching apothecary.

"I can smell it on you," Noname said. "Your whole body reeks of blood. It's been a long time since I've smelled that scent so strongly. What a pretty little face too." In the blink of an eye, she was right in front of Suimei and leaning in close to sniff his neck. "So how many have you killed?"

"Hah!" he cried. Right at that moment, Suimei swiped up a shard from one of the broken bottles on the floor and swung it at Noname's neck.

"Oh, come now," she said, easily dodging. "Tooooo bad."

Noname shrank back before launching her long arm out like a striking viper. In a blink, she had Suimei's wrist and used it to twist his whole arm. He yelped as he dropped the glass and cried out in pain.

"You're a lively one. That's good in a kid," she purred.

I could only gape at this whole display. Noname, who'd always been like a mother to me, closed in on Suimei quicker than I could blink. Was she actually going to kill him? It was plain to all that she could, if she so desired. He would be unable to defend himself. I could do little but stand back in shock and fret. I was worried for *both* of them.

Meanwhile, Noname let out a piercing laugh as blood dripped from Suimei's hand. "Well, that won't do. Looks like you cut yourself on that glass. I guess I'll have to fix you up all over again." A chilling smile curled across Noname's lips. She stroked Suimei's wrist. "Let's put some medicine on that, shall we?"

Sweat beaded Suimei's brow as Noname leaned in close with a warm smile on her lips. She spoke in a low, sweet voice dripping with scorn. "I think we're done, don't you?"

He remained silent, but it was clear that he was out of options. Suimei closed his eyes. "Kill me then."

Whoa, wait a second! I slapped Noname with all the strength I could muster. "Get a hold of yourself!"

"Ouch!" Noname cried out in surprise—at least I got her to let go of Suimei's wrist. "I was just kidding!"

"You went way beyond joking," I scolded. "He lives with me now, okay? It's thanks to him that I can finally eat nice food."

"Well, you don't say," she murmured. "I'm sorry, kiddo, I was just testing you. Shinonome's a soft old fool, you know, so I figured I'd see what you were really about."

"Really, now," Suimei grumbled.

"Of course." Noname returned to her chipper self as she brushed the dust off Suimei's clothes. "I need to know these things. It's for Kaori, after all. A parent's love, you could say. Listen, I'd really appreciate it if you'd forgive me for all this."

"I have to admit, it's been a while since I've had to actually get serious like that—you're good. Fast. Quite a strong one, all in all, and I can tell that you held back. What a shame." She brought her hand to her mouth and chuckled. "Well, you don't seem like a bad kid. Just remember to stick with Nyaa-san or Kaori when wandering around the spirit realm. You never know when you'll run across another spirit with a nose like mine. You're human, after all. You stand out around here. At least until people think of you as a Strangeling like Kaori."

Finally, Noname eased off, heading to the back of the shop to find something to help with Suimei's bleeding.

"Well, that's a relief," I sighed. For a moment there, I'd really worried I was about to see some sort of spirit versus exorcist showdown. Once Suimei was properly taken care of, we'd go back to my house and relax...or so I'd hoped. Before we could retreat, someone wrapped their arms around me from behind.

"Y-you're an exorcist?!" Ginme said. I couldn't tell if Ginme was trying to protect me, but he held me close as he glared daggers at Suimei.

"That's correct," Suimei said.

"And you've slain a bunch of spirits?"

"I guess so."

"What are you doing here? Are you here to kill someone?"

"No, I'm just looking for someone is all."

Oh, no. Was this going to lead to another fight? Suimei was being way too frank now that the secret was out. My stomach knotted as the tension in the room ramped back up.

Fortunately, Kinme spoke up, his tone calm and casual. "Huh, you only figured that out just now, Ginme? I mean, Suimei looks exactly like an exorcist."

"What?! You knew?" Ginme gasped.

Kinme shrugged and wagged a confident finger. "Man, you're a real idiot. You should really think harder about why a human wouldn't be scared of us. Also, he didn't show the least bit of interest in the strange world around him."

Ginme pouted before letting out a dramatic sigh and slumping his shoulders. "You should tell me these things sooner..."

Suimei frowned as well. "So you saw right through me, then."

Now both Ginme and Suimei looked dejected. They were more alike than either would ever admit.

Ginme suddenly perked back up. "Heh, I guess I kinda got ahead of myself. Pretty foolish, huh? I mean, who cares if you're an exorcist, Suimei? If Shinonome and Noname have vouched for you, then it doesn't matter what I think. Besides, we're friends!"

Ah, good old Ginme, always ready to look on the bright side of things.

"I *have* slain many spirits, you know," Suimei said.

"Eh, I bet they were all doing bad stuff in the human world, right?" Ginme countered. "You reap what you sow. And what's any of that got to do with the here and now?"

Ginme offered a toothy grin. I had to admire his ability to just let things go. He and his brother had matured into admirable young adults. I slipped out of his arms and stood on my tiptoes to pat his head. "You've really grown up into a good kid, you know," I said.

"Hey, cut it out! Don't treat me like a child," Ginme said.

"I'm sorry," Suimei cut in. "But—I still can't be friends with you."

"Why not?" I blurted out.

"I'm not allowed to have emotions," Suimei said simply. "Therefore, I can't make friends."

What the heck was that supposed to mean? Noname spared me from having to respond to that when she returned with snacks, tea, and medicine.

"We can talk about whatever this is later," she sang. "I've brought snacks."

She insisted that we all sit down, and served up some traditional Chinese tea and mooncakes. Noname hummed to herself as she tended to Suimei's hand but broke off her tune when she realized no one was eating. It fell to me to explain the strange tension in the room.

"Well, well. Many of these old multi-generational professions involve certain self-imposed restrictions," she mused. "It's not like anyone enjoyed restraining themselves in this or that regard, it was just how things were. I suppose the need to stifle your emotions is a side effect of the abilities exorcists rely on to do their jobs. Friends always seem to find a way to affect your emotional state, so if you intend to continue on as an exorcist, I suppose friendships are best avoided. They would only ever plague you with unnecessary feelings."

What an interesting restriction. It seemed there was a lot more to being an exorcist than just dealing with spirits.

"Wow, that sounds tough," I said. "Hey, Suimei, now that I think about it, you mentioned earlier that you'd closed up shop. Do you still plan on being an exorcist even after finding whatever you're looking for?"

Suimei froze, weighing each word before responding in a whisper. "That...I really don't know."

"In that case, there's nothing wrong with making friends, right?"

"I...I guess so. But it's not that simple." Suimei fell silent, sullenly sizing up everyone around him. He almost looked as if he were afraid of something.

He was, after all, forced to constantly bottle up his emotions since he was a young boy. Whether he wanted them or not, emotions were part of being human. How difficult must it have been to live his whole life denying what he felt?

I finally understood why Suimei had seemed so conflicted during breakfast. He must have spent most of his life limiting his interactions with other people in order to keep his emotions in check. Sitting around the breakfast table with such a large group had been galling. It all just struck me as sad. The boy in front of me was as yet still burdened by the heavy chains that had bound him for so long.

I'd been incredibly insensitive.

"Kaori, stop trying to force him." Noname said.

"Right..." My shoulders slumped. She was right.

"It's not that I don't understand, of course," Noname went on. "Just that there's no need to rush anything. And that goes for both of you, Kaori, Suimei. Listen, Exorcist Boy, you're in the spirit realm now. No one's going to judge the choices you make, so just live however you wish. If a little emotion comes out here or there, I don't see anything wrong with that."

Suimei remained silent, though his gaze wavered with uncertainty. He had finally been freed from the burden he'd lived under since the day of his birth. I could only imagine how hard it had to be to turn your back on something that had been etched into your psyche for your whole life.

Maybe it was fate that Suimei and I had crossed paths. Deep in my heart, I knew that I wanted to help him.

"I'm really sorry for not thinking of your situation, Suimei," I said. "I hope you find the spirit you're looking for. If there's anything I can do to help, please let me know."

"Hey, we'll help too!" Ginme declared. "We've got time on our hands."

"We've got training, Ginme..." Kinme chided him.

"Huh? What? I can't hear you."

"You're just using this as an excuse to slack off."

"Pretty much!"

We all broke out in laughter before Suimei spoke up, a perplexed look on his face.

"Why are you all looking out for me?"

The brothers and I exchanged looks before nodding in unison.

"Well, Shinonome-san and Noname always taught me to help those in need," I said.

"Now that I think about it, becoming friends is something that just kind of naturally happens," Suimei snorted. "Trying to push someone into it is kind of rude."

"What can I say, we like to meddle." I grinned. "And it's not just us. Most of the people in town are the same."

Kinme smirked. "The spirits who hang around Kaori tend to care for those in their inner circle. You should probably get used to the idea, in case you're ever accepted as a Strangeling too. You probably won't be able to avoid making friends."

Red washed through Suimei's face. He turned his gaze down toward the table and mumbled to himself.

"Aah, the joys of youth," Noname said. "If I were just two thousand years younger... Anyway, if you have any worries or problems, please just stop on by."

Just then a dark figure slunk into the shop.

"Meeeow." Nyaa brushed against my legs and plopped down on the floor. "Hey, Kaori, Nurarihyon asked that we go and deliver a book to him, and, well, obviously you're the one who's going to go do it. While you're at it, be sure to pick up the other book he borrowed, since it's nearing its due date."

"Nurarihyon?" I frowned. "But why can't he come here on his own? He always brings some little present with him when he stops by."

"Who knows? Busy, I guess."

Nurarihyon held some sway among the spirits. He would enter other spirits' houses as he pleased and make himself at home with tea and snacks. He was also an avid reader and therefore a longtime customer of ours. He often stopped by to borrow a hefty haul of books to take home with him. For someone who didn't really seem to do much on his own, it seemed odd for him to be busy.

My frown deepened. "This is weird. I'm kind of worried. Let's get going."

"Hey," Suimei interjected before we could leave. "So now your haunted bookstore makes home deliveries too? Don't you think you're overdoing it with the extra services?"

What was he getting at?

I puffed out my chest with pride. "As the only bookstore in the spirit realm, home delivery is just one of the many services we provide to ensure that books can be read by all spirits with an interest in stories."

"You know, Shinonome said that it really isn't necessary," Nyaa-san sniffed.

"Hmph. Anywhere in Japan, that's our motto."

"And I'm the one who gets dragged along for the ride."

Way to hit me where it hurts, Nyaa-san!

The bird twins had tears in their eyes from barely restrained laughter. "Great job, Nyaa-senpai. We don't know how you do it!" they said in unison.

"Hmph. Oh well, I guess this is the lot I drew in life when we met," Nyaa-san sighed.

Okay, so maybe she wasn't exactly wrong. I pretty much dragged Nyaa-san everywhere I went, working up a good sweat along the way and then stopping by Noname's for help.

Noname pulled out some dried sardines and offered them to Nyaa-san as some kind of reward for all her hard work. Jeez, was hanging out with me really that tough? At this rate, I'd be the one with no friends, not Suimei.

"We're...we're best friends, aren't we, Nyaa-san?" I asked, eyes welling with tears. "You're still going to join me on my jobs, right?"

Nyaa-san licked her nose, her three tails wagging. "Of course. No one else but me would follow you on all your crazy adventures."

"Aww, Nyaa-san, I love you!"

"Meow?! Meeeeooooowwww!"

I pulled Nyaa-san into a tight—perhaps too tight—embrace and earned several fresh scratches in response.

The following day, after all the drama at the apothecary's, we headed to the human world to make our delivery.

Fujiyoshida, in Yamanashi Prefecture, served up a clear sky the day we went in search of Nurarihyon. We stepped into a gorgeous afternoon flooded with sunlight. I could just imagine Nyaa-san finding a nearby rooftop and plopping down for an afternoon nap.

Suimei, on the other hand, looked glum. At first I thought it was just him suppressing his emotions, but something told me that he was in a genuinely bad mood. The sulky expression ruined his otherwise attractive face.

I slurped down my udon noodles while pondering the issue. We were eating in a restaurant that had once been the first floor of a home. A remodel had turned the place into an eatery serving one of Fujiyoshida's most famous dishes. Because of the shop's original architecture, eating there gave one the domestic feeling of visiting a friend or relative.

A bowl of Yoshida udon sat before me now, brimming with horse meat stewed in sweet and spicy stock, accompanied by vegetable tempura, and topped with burdock. The land in Fujiyoshida wasn't suitable for cultivating rice, so wheat was the staple food in this region. Houtou, a noodle soup made with udon noodles and vegetables, was probably the most famous wheat-based dish to come out of Yamanashi, but this Yoshida udon was well known in its own right. The broth, made of a mixture of soy sauce and miso, left one feeling refreshed. The thickness of the noodles rivaled even that of the more famous Sanuki udon and were cut with squared sides, like elongated rectangles, which give them a hearty mouthfeel.

I slurped noisily and let out a blissful sigh. The center of the noodles was still quite firm, which really allowed the wheat to shine. Chew, blast of flavor, chew, blast of flavor. Even if you couldn't really enjoy it on the way down, it made the chewing process immensely satisfying. Whenever you got tired of that, you could add in some of the spicy base for more zing, creating a whole new delicious flavor profile with the heat.

"This meat udon is awesome," Ginme enthused.

"I love the inari sushi," Kinme agreed.

Suimei fixed the twins with an annoyed glare. "Spirits shouldn't get too used to eating out here in the human world."

"What's wrong with it?" Kinme said. "Besides, as far as the humans are concerned, we look just like them."

"Exactly," Ginme said. "As long as no one notices, we'll be fine."

The twins had dressed for the occasion to make them look a bit more human. Kinme wore a thin sweater and slacks while Ginme had on a hoodie and chino pants. They used a Tengu ability to disguise their feet—their dead giveaway—and now they looked like any other guy. None of this appeased Suimei, however, and he frowned at his food.

"Why are we sitting around eating udon if the whole point of coming here was to deliver a book?" he asked.

"Well, I mean, it's lunchtime," Ginme said.

"We came all the way out to Yamanashi, right?" Kinme added. "And if you're out in Fujiyoshida, then Yoshida udon is pretty much the thing you eat."

"Hey, we should go through Izu on the way back and have some fresh sardines while we're there," Ginme said.

"What, are we tourists now?" Suimei groaned.

I struggled not to laugh. For all Suimei's talk of denying his emotions, he was getting quite animated. But even more so, it just made me happy to see him actively engaging in conversation.

Despite my best efforts, my amusement apparently showed on my face. One look at me and Suimei instantly scowled. "What's with your face? You look hideous."

"Hey, that's a little rude, don't you think?"

Far from apologizing, Suimei simply changed the subject. "Anyway, why'd you bring me here in the first place?"

"Huh?"

Come to think of it, he had a point. To be fair, he couldn't exactly travel around the spirit realm without an escort. I'd figured he'd be bored if we left him behind. But this was Suimei we were talking about. If I told him that I'd brought him along on a whim, he'd undoubtedly get mad, so I scrambled for a plausible explanation.

"Well, when you travel, you need companions," I said.

"What kind of justification is that?"

Okay, maybe that was a bit too out there. Suimei sighed but let the topic drop, turning back to his bowl and reluctantly slurping up his noodles. Much to my surprise, however, he seemed to enjoy himself. At least his eyes softened somewhat. Good food has a way of soothing the soul. I focused on my own meal as well.

While Suimei was still eating, the rest of us spread out a map of Mount Fuji.

"You know, I never figured that this year was gonna be the one when the cycle came around again," Kinme mused.

"I know. The major spirits should all be off on their travels," I agreed.

"It's pretty amusing that your bookstore would have such a useful book in it, dontcha think?"

"How so?"

Suimei perked up at this, which was fair considering that he was the only one who didn't know what we were talking about. His mouth was still full of noodles, even as he glared, demanding to know what was going on.

"Are you familiar with Daidarabotchi?" I asked.

He inclined his head. "The legendary giant, right?"

"That's right, a giant. A real big one. Daidarabotchi travels all across Japan, you see, over the course of many years and months. Obviously, normal people can't see him, though."

Noname had told me about Daidarabotchi a long time ago. There was something strange and special about Daidarabotchi's body that made him incredibly terrifying to those who saw him. Daidarabotchi could pass right through solid objects but could also affect those he decided to crash into. His path around Japan was influenced both by the direction of the winds and his own flights of fancy. He was a rather uninhibited spirit in that regard.

The majority of the information surrounding the legend of Daidarabotchi could be attributed to the Edo-era Confucian scholar Oka Hakku and his work, *A Humorous Study of Curious Tales*, featuring the legends of the place then known as Oumi. For some reason, Daidarabotchi had carved up the land of

Oumi and piled the resulting dirt into large mounds. These mounds had ultimately become Mount Fuji while the earth that was dug away had become Lake Biwa. He had also plopped down other large masses of earth as he went, creating yet more mountains along his path.

"It seems like Daidarabotchi will be passing by Mount Fuji pretty soon," I said. "Do you know why Daidarabotchi made Mount Fuji in the first place?"

"Why would I know that?" Suimei asked. There was no reason why he would. After all, I only knew it by dumb luck.

"He figured it'd be a great place to take a nap."

"Huh?"

"Look, see the Izu Peninsula over there?" I pointed on the map. "That's perfect for stretching your legs out. He made Mount Fuji as his pillow. That's what Noname told me."

Suimei's face went blank as he stared silently into the distance. Maybe he didn't understand what I was saying? I tried a different approach.

"Daidarabotchi, you see, he chose Fuji as a place to rest. Apparently, there was a time when he just couldn't sleep. He kept tossing and turning, which is what caused Mount Fuji to erupt. In order to make sure that doesn't happen again, Nurarihyon helps him fall asleep. Remember the book? Well, that's why Nurarihyon called us here."

"Huh, so you've met Daidarabotchi?" Suimei gaped.

"Nope, it's my first time! But I'm kind of nervous. He must be huge, right?"

The book Nurarihyon had asked us to bring was incredibly important not only to our store but to me as well. For starters, it really did put people to sleep, and since we didn't want Mount Fuji erupting, that was a big deal. So while I understood Nurarihyon might have had trouble getting to our store, we had a duty to get this book into his hands.

"Daidarabotchi should arrive at Mount Fuji by dawn," I explained. "I'm positive that's where we'll find Nurarihyon. We might as well start our search there."

"Uh, hey," Suimei said. "Dawn is quite a long ways away, you know. I mean, it's noon now. What do you plan on doing 'til then?"

The twins and I shared a look and smirked. I pulled a pamphlet out of my bag and spread it out on top of the map. "We're going to the amusement park, of course. I finally got someone to cover my shift at work, so I might as well enjoy my day off to the fullest."

"I'm gonna ride the world's fastest roller coaster!" Ginme crowed.

"I want to try my hand at the super scary maze." Kinme grinned. "Apparently it takes a whole fifty minutes just to make it through the haunted house. I wonder how scary it really is?"

"This is gonna be great. Oh—what's up, Suimei?" I glanced at him.

Suimei had lowered his head to the table. When I shook him by the shoulder, he didn't respond at all.

"Well, if you're not gonna finish your bowl, I'll have the rest of it." Ginme reached for the udon.

"No!" Suimei bolted back up to snatch it back.

Suimei eventually finished his meal, and we all headed out, traveling toward Fuji-Q Highland for a day of amusements.

Afterward, we headed on to our mission with Nyaa-san as she padded through the night sky on legs wreathed in fire. Suimei and I sat on her back while Ginme and Kinme flew beside us.

"Hnngh..." Suimei groaned.

"You okay?" I asked.

Suimei slumped on Nyaa-san's back. Sweat poured down his pale face.

"You're pretty weak for an exorcist, you know," Nyaa-san said.

"Shut up, cat," he grumbled.

He hadn't taken well to a day of roller coasters. I dabbed his forehead with a damp handkerchief and peered down at the expansive Kofu Basin, said to have been made by Daidarabotchi himself. I smiled at the thought of the giant digging around like a child in a sandbox, scrounging up enough dirt to build Mount Fuji.

As dawn was nearing, most of the homes below stood dark. Occasionally, we'd pass a row of orderly streetlights, or a car would go flashing past like a comet streaking across the ground. All these ordinary, human things reminded me that we were in their world, where humans were meant to live; we weren't in the spirit realm anymore... I shook my head free of the thought and gazed into the distance.

The tremendous bulk of Mount Fuji reared up ahead. Japan's tallest mountain lorded over the Kofu Basin, hulking over humanity below. I searched for Nurarihyon, but I didn't see him, Daidarabotchi, or any other spirit for that matter.

I began to worry as a haze of light indicated the sun nearing the horizon.

"This is the correct spot, right, Kinme?" I asked. "He should be on the Shizuoka side of the mountain, yeah?"

"Yup, apparently Daidarabotchi is coming from Suwa. So this should be it."

"This is the right place, Kaori," a man's voice agreed.

I jerked toward the sound and found a white, puffy appendage in my face. Blue light radiated off of jellyfish tentacles buzzing with electricity. Countless more tentacles fluttered in the wind.

"Nurarihyon-sama!" The twins called out in unison as they bowed their heads in respect. "It's been too long."

"Oho, boys, I see you've made it." The figure of Nurarihyon stood beneath the jellyfish like it were an umbrella. It wagged its tentacles as if in greeting as Nurarihyon belted out a laugh. "Sorry for making you come all the way out here, Kaori."

The preeminent spirit could have passed for a man in his thirties, but he spoke like someone much, much older. His traditional monk scarf seemed oddly out of place on a jellyfish, even if this form was only temporary. Nurarihyon didn't have a "true" form, so to speak, and he changed every time we met. Truly a man, er, spirit of mystery.

"Let me give these back to you before we continue." Nurarihyon stretched out one of his jellyfish's tendrils toward me. It carried several books, all nearing their due dates.

"Looks like everything's in order," I said, taking the stack of books. "And here's the book you asked me for. Can you make sure it's the right one?"

"Of course."

I pulled out an old book bound in the traditional Japanese style. Intricate symbols decorated the cover and gave the whole thing an otherworldly appearance. As soon as Nurarihyon saw it, he smiled.

"Oh ho ho, my thanks, Kaori, for bringing me such an invaluable book. I'll just need it for tonight."

I nodded. "Okay!"

Nurarihyon accepted the book. As he moved, the gaps in his midnight blue scarf and monk robes revealed a tiny jellyfish peeking out. Having confirmed this was the book he needed, Nurarihyon smiled, his eyes crinkling as his gray hair wafted in the wind. "This will definitely put Daidarabotchi down gently."

"You make it sound like he's going to die!"

"Ah, my apologies. Let's just keep that slip-up between us." Nurarihyon winked one brown eye and brought a finger up to his lips. His cheeks softened in an almost human smile.

Finally, I voiced the question that'd been bothering me. "So where *is* Daidarabotchi?"

"Huh? Oh, right. Didn't Noname tell you? Daidarabotchi is that way."

Just then, a massive, black figure appeared behind Nurarihyon. It was so huge it blocked my view of anything else.

"Eyagh!" I swallowed hard.

This was the first time I'd ever seen Daidarabotchi. He was massive, a black form composed entirely of shadows. While he looked almost human, the darkness shrouding him obscured any sense of depth. It was like looking at an endless sheet of paper drenched in calligraphy ink, a pure shadow so immense it could shake the heavens and move mountains. The mere sight of him left me in awe.

I swallowed again in an attempt to moisten my suddenly parched throat. Despite having lived the majority of my life in the spirit realm, I was terrified of this titanic spirit I knew so little about. I glanced at the twins, but they didn't seem the least bit bothered. It was too much for me, though. I trembled before the giant.

At times like this, I usually curled up by Shinonome-san's side until the feeling passed, but he wasn't here right now. I had to weather this on my own. I clenched my jaw to fight back the tears.

Alas, despite my best efforts, my vision blurred. In all my time in the spirit realm, there were only two things I couldn't stand: One was when the glimmerflies swarmed around me, and the other was the spirits who evoked true mortal terror.

I liked to think I had the body of a human but the heart of a spirit. I'd even said as much to Suimei. But an event like this left me feeling incredibly, painfully human. Sure, I'd grown to love the spirit realm, even to feel I belonged there. But in truth, I'd been shoved out of the human world, forcibly removed. So where did I really belong?

"Haaaaaah." I let out a long breath and tried to pretend everything was okay. If I were a spirit, this situation wouldn't be scary at all. But no matter how much I tried to fit in among the rest of them, my human mind rang every alarm bell it had at the sight of this hulking presence. The mix of fear and confusion made me want to bolt.

I slumped on Nyaa-san's back—until someone warm reached out to hold me. Suimei. Even though he'd been so pale just moments ago, now he was the one sitting up straight and steadying me as I wavered.

"Th-thanks," I managed.

Suimei just shook his head. "There are many more stories about Daidarabotchi, but I'd always written them off as mere folklore. Honestly, I only half believed you when you told me about him, Kaori." His breath blew warm against me as he went on excitedly. "So Daidarabotchi's real. He's huge...and frightening."

"Frightening?" I craned my neck to blink at Suimei.

"Of course. Just look, I'm shaking."

Now that he mentioned it, I was trembling too.

Suimei's simple comment, his attempt to support me—it completely wiped away the fear racking my body, like sunlight burning through the morning mist. The knowledge that another person shared my fear brought with it a sort of comfort.

I turned all the way around to face Suimei. "Well, if you're scared, do you want me to give you hug?"

His whole face changed. "No way, idiot."

"Aw, no need to be modest. Let me take care of you."

"Once you start properly acting your age, then maybe you can talk like that."

"I guess you've got a point."

Though Suimei still eyed Daidarabotchi, he no longer trembled as he had. I kind of hoped that I'd been of some help in turn. I faced Daidarabotchi myself, feeling much steadier as I sized up the massive black form.

"He's huge..." I murmured.

"I wonder if he's going to attack us..." Suimei muttered.

"No way. Nurarihyon's here."

As Suimei and I talked, Nurarihyon finally got to work. First, he skimmed over Daidarabotchi's head, twisting his jellyfish tendrils as he went. Daidarabotchi reached up for him, like a giant toddler grasping for a toy dangling from a mobile.

After playing with Daidarabotchi for a time, Nurarihyon spoke gently to the giant down below. "Well, well, you've been walking for some time," he said. "You must be tired. Kaori brought this book, you know, so why don't I read you a bedtime story? Climb on into your Fuji cradle and take a short rest."

Nurarihyon opened the book, and a bright light shone from the pages, illuminating everything around us. "Well, then, Daidarabotchi, today I'm going to read you the 'Tale of the Bamboo Cutter.'"

No sooner had the words left his mouth than a semi-transparent bamboo forest made of light appeared in the air, created by the book in Nurarihyon's hand.

An old man strolled through the illusory bamboo forest, obviously the fabled bamboo cutter. As soon as he spotted a glowing stalk of bamboo, he cut into it, at which his eyes flew wide with shock. A beautiful princess sprang from the bamboo stalk.

Just then, someone tugged on my sleeve.

"What?" I whispered.

"Is that some kind of hologram?" Suimei asked.

"Can't you see it's a picture book? It's pretty normal for pictures to come out of them, you know."

"Yeah, but not like that! You sure have a strange outlook on things."

While Suimei was busy complaining, the scene above us shifted with the story. Every time the image floating in the air changed, Daidarabotchi reached up to touch it.

"Sorry, most books aren't like this," I assured Suimei. "This one was made specially by Shinonome-san."

"Hmph, all right. But I have to admit, this is pretty impressive. You could probably make a fortune if you sold it."

"This book is a one of a kind—a miracle. We couldn't make another one if we wanted to. So we'd be in a real bind if we sold it."

"That's right," Kinme added, pulling up by our side. "Shinonome-san made this book especially to get this little crybaby Kaori here to feel better. If he sold this book, Kaori'd kill him. Noname told me *all* about it. When she was a little kid, she'd cry at the slightest breeze or noise whenever she went outside, or even when it was time to eat. It's like she was an endless well of tears—she'd keep crying until her clothes were sopping wet!"

"C'mon, Kinme, cut it out!" I protested.

Nurarihyon floated over, drawn by our conversation.

"At the time, all sorts of spirits stopped by the bookstore to come gawk at the little crybaby. Even I stopped by," Kinme said.

"Spirits just love a good marvel, don't they?" Nurarihyon said with a snicker.

To be fair, it was all true: I really had been a crybaby.

Back when I was little, I'd cried at the slightest provocation, no matter what had happened or where I was. To be fair, I'd grown up in a world of constant darkness, chased by butterflies and living among all manner of creepy spirit beings. It was a bit intense for a human child.

Shinonome-san had been at his wits' end when he put his head together with Noname to make this picture book we were reading from today. From then on, whenever I'd start crying, they would pull out this very book and tell me the story. I would become so entranced by the images floating in the air that I'd forget about crying almost immediately. Even Shinonome-san would crack a smile seeing me calm down and giggle.

"Well, thanks to that rough time, they conjured a brilliant book that can project its stories," Nurarihyon said. "It's a one-of-a-kind, priceless artifact made just for Kaori. And it puts Daidarabotchi to sleep like nothing else. Sometimes I dread the ordeal of trying to get him to rest, but then I remember this book and ask Shinonome-san for it."

The jellyfish's tendrils held Daidarabotchi to the ground until he was properly lulled, just like a swaddled infant. I smiled as I imagined Nurarihyon struggling with this unruly, childish spirit.

This book created just for me held the power to help him too. Every time someone opened it, I was filled with new strength, a sense of comfort washing over me.

However, since I'd reached adulthood, I'd rarely ever had an opportunity to look through it. It just sat on the shelf, filed away, and I had worried it would stay that way, gathering dust. "It seems a waste for this book to belong only to me," I said. "I'm really glad that it can bring such joy to Daidarabotchi too."

Nurarihyon brushed my head with one of his tendrils. "My, my. I can definitely say that Shinonome's hard work paid off. He really raised you right."

"Aww, c'mon, Nurarihyon, don't pat my head like that in front of people. It's embarrassing!"

My face flushed pink, and Nurarihyon chuckled, bringing his jellyfish body in close to my burning cheek to cool it. I turned my gaze downward as soft, cool, springy jellyfish flesh brushed against my cheek. That's how I noticed that Daidarabotchi was resting his head on Mount Fuji, absently watching the images playing out before him. He looked like he could fall asleep at any moment.

For an instant, I panicked at the thought of all the homes that would be crushed underneath his body. But when I looked closer, I noticed cars passing straight through him like he wasn't even there.

"Aww, drift, drift off to sleep. Right here, atop the immortal mount. Drift, drift to sleep," Nurarihyon sang. He patted Daidarabotchi with one of his tendrils as he cooed the lullaby. The massive spirit's eyes drooped shut.

"Hey, Kaori," Suimei said.

"What is it?"

"Was the spirit realm really so scary to you that you cried constantly? Didn't you ever just think about coming back?"

The sun finally crested the horizon, bringing with it a gentle white sheen that drove away the darkness. As the shadows receded, color brightened the land below. It would have been beautiful, but...

My mind flashed back to the sound of water, distorted vision, the sensation of suffocating.

The black shadow that uttered the curse that sent me down into the water.

I held my breath and squeezed my eyes shut, pushing the memory back and forcing a smile. "Do...do I look that unhappy?"

Suimei blinked several times before shaking his head.

"Right!" I mussed his white hair. "To be honest, I actually don't have any memories of the human world from before I ended up in the spirit realm. My whole life, everything I've ever experienced—it all happened with the spirits. That's where I belong. So if someone told me to go back, well..."

Right then, the conclusion to "Tale of the Bamboo Cutter" was playing out across the sky.

The emperor brought his forces to protect Princess Kaguya from those trying to bring her back to her original home. Despite his efforts, the people of the moon still managed to snatch her away and drag her there. Though she left behind a letter describing how to make a medicine that would grant the emperor eternal life, the moment she donned her heavenly robes, she forgot all of the warmth and compassion she'd received from her family and the other people of earth.

The entourage from the moon, as they appeared in the book's description, were absolutely stunning. Their gilded ox-cart cut through the sky on its way back to the heavens, glimmering as it went. Though Princess Kaguya, riding in the back of the carriage, had no expression, her tears glistened in the light of the moon as she rose higher and higher into the sky.

"If someone told me to go back, I'd refuse," I concluded. "I'd stay in the spirit realm instead, working in the bookstore and just enjoying the life I have there."

"I see," Suimei murmured.

I smirked at Suimei before finally straightening out his messy hair. "You're a nice kid, Suimei."

"What makes you say that?"

I smiled as Suimei fell silent. Something silver flashed in my peripheral vision, and then Ginme tugged on my arm.

"Hey, what's with you guys getting all close like that?" Ginme prodded.

"Cut it out!" I batted him away. "O-oh, no!"

The force of Ginme's tug had sent me tumbling off Nyaa-san's back. I screamed for my life, breaking out in a cold sweat as I plummeted.

I jerked to a stop after only a second.

"Are you okay?!" Ginme gasped.

He and Suimei each held me by one hand while Kinme clung to one leg and Nyaa-san wrapped her tail around the other. Nurarihyon even had a tendril around my waist.

With everyone's help, I made it back onto Nyaa-san's back.

Nyaa-san growled at Ginme once I was safely aboard. "Ginme, you idiot! What would you do if something had happened to Kaori?!"

"Eep! I'm sorry, Nyaa-san!"

"Listen, my little brother here really wasn't thinking," Kinme apologized.

Nyaa-san sighed, but I just laughed the whole thing off. "I have to admit, I was pretty terrified for a moment there!"

It seemed like I was the only one with any cheer to spare, though. Everyone else was still tense about the fall. I realized then that if I *were* Princess Kaguya, and if the people of the moon did come to steal me away, my friends probably would do everything they could to chase after me. To be fair, I wouldn't go willingly either, or without a fight. I'd do whatever it took to stay home— the home I'd chosen. I was one of the spirits, after all.

Warmth spread through my chest at the thought. I looked down at the sleeping Daidarabotchi, equally content among his friends.

"Look..." I nodded toward him.

He'd fallen asleep right as the fairy tale ended. Daidarabotchi went translucent in the light of the morning sun. His body refracted the beams like a crystal, too brilliant to look at directly but so beautiful I felt compelled to try anyway. Everyone fell silent as they took in the sight.

My heart was racing, and my body trembled. What an honor it was to be here to witness something like this.

After some time, Daidarabotchi melded together with the sky in a prism of light, though I knew deep down that we merely couldn't see him anymore and that he was still slumbering peacefully at the base of Mount Fuji. Once he awoke, he would continue his trek around Japan. It must be so freeing to travel like that, wandering wherever his mood took him.

Nurarihyon handed the book back to me. "Thank you. I think we should be fine for now."

I hugged the book to my chest. "I hope we were of some help?"

Nurarihyon's eyes crinkled with mirth. He reached out to pat me on the head. "Of course you were. I'm sure I'll have another favor to ask of you sometime soon."

I beamed brightly and nodded. "Any time you need anything, call on the haunted bookstore!"

Nurarihyon smiled. "That I shall."

Even Spirits Dream of Summer

MY MOTHER always looked quite pale.

I had a distinct memory of her sitting atop her futon in a Japanese tatami room, brushing out her long black hair, which was as dark as a starless night. The comb made it shine and drew out my mother's true beauty. She generally maintained a rather neutral expression, though I recall her face softening at the end of the day when she brushed out her hair like this.

As a child, watching her, I sat transfixed, forgetting all about my wooden block toys. My mother smiled when she noticed me. I brightened and smiled myself at this rare show of emotion, but her face quickly hardened again. She waved me over with a pale hand and pulled me into a warm embrace. "You can't smile, you know, not outside."

"Why?"

"Bad things will happen to you."

"Huh?"

Mother was always telling me to rid myself of my emotions, insisting that I didn't need them to live. You see, emotions were expressly forbidden for members of the Inugami Demon line. Happiness, anger, sadness, fun—all of these emotions could in some way result in jealousy.

Inugami was a tsukimono, a possessing power that had been created using techniques similar to those of a shaman or other like practitioner. But Inugami's creation had been both horrifying and cruel, and the family it was tied to would be forever known as a "tsukimono clan." Our tsukimono, Inugami, had brought great blessings to its bound family. However, if someone who belonged to Inugami felt envy toward someone or something, it would bring great suffering to that subject—cursing it with illness, pain, and ruin.

You must not feel. That was life for those born into a tsukimono clan, whose obligation was to perform exorcisms for the sake of society.

"That's our lot in life," Mother said. This was a phrase she often used. She stroked the strange creature on her lap and sighed. "You must be strong. Any time you feel lonely, or like you might lose control of yourself, just pull Inugami close and sleep."

After she said this, she called a servant to remove me from her room.

That was the last time I ever saw her. For the six months following, I was forced to live in a pitch-black room in order to better enable me to suppress my emotions. Only after those six months did I learn of my mother's passing.

"Hey, partner. I guess that means you're my master now," the creature said.

A bit long for a dog, it had black fur and red spots. It almost looked like a weasel with an elongated face and pointed ears. It bared its teeth in a kind of smile before rubbing its body up against me affectionately.

"Suimei! Wake up, it's time for breakfast," Kaori called.

As always, the spirit realm lay dark. A glimmerfly skimmed past my face. I rubbed at my head to try to ease a throbbing headache and let out a deep breath. Reaching out unconsciously to my side, I suddenly tensed up—of course, he wasn't there. The pain in my head was an ever-present annoyance for me, but my missing companion was a far larger concern.

He was gone. That was the whole reason I'd even come to the spirit realm ten days ago.

He'd been by my side since my earliest memories. No matter how many dangerous trials I faced as an exorcist, he had always been with me, an irreplaceable asset.

My search had started in the human world, but I'd come up empty everywhere I looked. Left with no other options, I took my search to the spirit realm. Everything was going well up until I entered the abandoned shrine said to serve as a gateway at twilight. Apparently, one of the floorboards I stepped on had rotted through, and I tumbled down, smacking my head and losing consciousness in the process. Though I was lucky enough to have made it to the spirit realm, that fall could have easily been a fatal blow had Kaori not shown up and saved me. If it weren't for her, I'd probably have ended up as dinner.

"Suimei!" she called.

I rushed to get dressed. My headache finally began to subside as I shucked my oversized sleeping yukata. Small miracles. I threw on clothes and headed down the creaking stairs to find a familiar face waiting in the living room.

"Well, well, good morning, Suimei-chan," Noname cooed. "I made breakfast, but why don't you go on and wash your face first?"

At first glance, I felt like I was looking at an ageless fellow with matchless feminine charm... This was Noname, the apothecary, greeting me in an egregiously frilly white apron. My headache abruptly returned.

While I massaged my temples, Shinonome called out to me without looking up. "Sorry for the unsightly display this early in the morning, Suimei."

Shinonome might have pulled off the air of a distinguished, graying gentleman were it not for the unkempt facial hair. The horns didn't help either. Any second now, Kaori would kick off her morning routine of complaining about his negligent hygiene.

"How rude," Noname said. "Please pardon the dimwit."

"Oh, shut up. Haven't I told you to throw that apron out?" Shinonome muttered.

"But it suits me, doesn't it? Right, Kaori?" Noname said.

Kaori, her mouth full, offered a thumbs up. "This fried egg is amazing," she said when she could. "It's the perfect runniness—makes it so soft and gooey. Then there's the fresh green onions with just a touch of salt...ah, and the rice!"

"Aww, Kaori likes my cooking!" Noname said. "That wasn't exactly what I was looking for, but I'm happy all the same. Do you want more?"

"Hmm...maybe just a little." Kaori shyly pushed her empty bowl over for seconds.

This was the person who was, technically, my savior. Muramoto Kaori, a human girl with a brown bob, had ended up in the spirit realm by accident when she was a child and eventually saved me when I flailed my way into this realm as well.

I mumbled a greeting and headed to the well in the backyard, where I cranked up a wooden bucket full of cold water to wash my face. The humidity and heat of the past few nights had consistently left me sweaty when I woke up. Even worse, I'd just woken up from a nightmare and as a consequence was especially sticky.

I soaked a towel in the water before washing my face and body. It left me feeling refreshed and human again.

When I raised my face, I took in the everyday life of the spirit realm. It still looked nothing like I expected. The sky wasn't the typical clear blue but rather the hue shifted the longer I watched, leaving me with an uneasy feeling. Off in the distance, humanoid figures flew through the air. Human souls ascending? Then, when I looked past the fence, I saw a woman with an unusually elongated waist peeping into someone's house. Our eyes met, and I nodded before quickly averting my gaze.

"What was that about?" I muttered to myself.

My heart raced. I had to take several long breaths to calm myself. It seemed I still wasn't quite used to life here.

Ever since I was young, my elders had always warned me to never enter the spirit realm. It was full of terrifying spirits who would chew up any human who happened to stumble into their domain. Though this world certainly did have its surprises, I wondered what my elders would think if they saw how the spirits here went about their daily lives just like humans.

"Your food's gonna get cold if you don't hurry up, Suimei," Kaori called.

"Right."

I made my way back to the living room and took my place at the table. Today's breakfast was rice, Japanese-style fried eggs, broiled fish with pickled radish, miso soup with seaweed, and tea. Pretty much a traditional spread.

"I roasted up some small sausages just for you, Suimei-chan," Noname said to me. "You're a growing boy, so eat up."

She piled the sausages up next to the fish, eliciting a wide-eyed look from Shinonome.

"What?! Why only him?" Shinonome protested. "I don't need your stupid fish. Give me the sausages."

"I gave you one, didn't I, love? So shut your trap!"

"Am I not a growing boy too?!"

"With a face like that?"

"Shinonome-san loves meat more than anything," Kaori stage-whispered to me.

I grabbed my chopsticks, put my hands together, and blessed the food under my breath while they went on bantering.

I sipped the soup first. Seaweed floated in a base of boiled-down fish stock and miso. Though nothing really stood out about it, the soup radiated a gentle warmth that seeped through to my core, slowly waking me up. Back when I'd lived at home, we'd had a top-tier chef to prepare our food, so I was used to more extravagant meals. Still, for something so simple, it tasted incredible.

"So how is it, Suimei-chan?" Noname asked.

All eyes were on me. I looked down at the table and mumbled my response. "It's not bad."

Everyone's face lit up. I studied the table even harder, trying to hide my embarrassment. What was this strange feeling? I felt like something was swirling around deep inside me, warming me to the depths of my belly. There was something there, something I'd never known before.

I gazed to my side and felt a pang. Right. My companion still wasn't with me. For the rest of the morning, I couldn't quite shake that feeling of mingled loss and warmth.

"Hmm…rain."

Kaori's voice broke me out of my musing. The storms had abated somewhat as we exited the rainy season, or so I'd hoped. Just then, a downpour erupted. It mingled with the humidity to create a muggy, uncomfortable haze of damp heat. The unpaved road outside quickly turned into a slurry of mud that I could smell even from the table.

Apparently, spirits also didn't much care for the rain, because barely anyone came to the shop that day. It was my turn to watch over the shop. Under any normal circumstances, I could have used the lull to go search for my friend, but Kaori stopped me, explaining that I'd stick out like a sore thumb. If I wanted to go anywhere, I needed an escort.

However, the only person I could ask to come with me was Kaori herself, and she'd gone off to work along with Nyaa. She wouldn't be back until lunch.

I sighed.

The smell of old paper and the glow of glimmerflies wafted through the empty bookstore. I still wondered how this place worked. The shelves were all so tall that I couldn't even see their tops, which didn't match up at all with the exterior. Somewhere above this room lay the guest room that I was sleeping in, but it was hard to believe that from looking upward.

Here was a world where you were never far from hell, one in which the human world's laws of physics were completely useless. In my boredom, I yearned to grab a ladder and try to scale one of these massive shelves, but it was just raw curiosity. Instead, I found some rare, old books bound in the traditional Japanese style: among them, the first part of Toriyama Sekien's *The Illustrated Demon Horde's Night Parade*. Though probably a copy, the book featured illustrations of various spirits. It had first been published in the fifth year of the An'ei era, 1776.

I flipped through the pages, wondering if spirits actually found some joy in looking through this book ostensibly about them. Or maybe they thought it was cute, or even quaint.

"Not a chance," I mumbled.

That was too ridiculous to dwell on. I returned the book and searched for another. From what I'd heard, this bookstore housed countless invaluable tomes. It even drew the curiosity of human researchers from time to time. Though the spirit realm and human world seemed irreconcilable, they were more closely intertwined than you might guess at first. Even as an exorcist, I hadn't quite appreciated the depth of the connection.

My mind was wandering. Too much free time.

The ceaseless rain left me depressed. I sat down and threw my legs forward. A glance into the main house revealed Shinonome struggling with a manuscript, smoke rising from his pipe. From what I'd been told, Shinonome had compiled quite a collection of stories from spirits over the years. Apparently, a number of enthusiasts out there were eager to buy these tales. He spent a lot of his downtime writing, claiming that it would one day add to the household budget.

"Gaah, damnable writer's block." Shinonome crumpled up a paper and tossed it away before starting again.

Despite knowing he'd saved Kaori, I knew surprisingly little about this elusive man. Judging by the horns protruding from his forehead and the scales on his cheeks, I suspected his human form was a ruse. I'd once asked him what he really was, but he had evaded the question and told me an exorcist should already know.

"Augh! I give up, I'm going to sleep!" Well, at least the way he squirmed around on the tatami floor reminded me of any other middle-aged human man. Obviously, I couldn't ask this guy to escort me around town. I hardly knew him, and I also didn't do well with father figures.

"I'm sure it can't be too bad if I stay close by," I murmured.

I turned to make my escape but regretted it when a baby the size of a small mountain lumbered in, drooling everywhere and blocking my exit.

"Human...smell good. Eat okay?" the baby said.

I fled to the back of the store. Ducking behind a bookshelf, I eyed the spirit as it wandered around for a bit before leaving. Only then did I breathe a sigh of relief.

I wiped the sweat from my forehead. As I relaxed, something caught my attention high up in the bookshelves. It moved like a spider, but upon closer inspection, I noticed its human face.

"Well, hello there, human," it said. "Have a moment?"

I swallowed hard and edged away from the spider. It skittered along, disappearing into a gap between the books. Okay, I was definitely not going out alone now. Instead, I found a feather duster and resigned myself to my duties around the store.

Plish. Plosh.

Raindrops pinged overhead as I dusted the books. I'd always loved the sound. The drumming of the raindrops echoed inside me, a soothing beat.

At length, the rain finally began to taper off. The perpetual darkness glowed just a little brighter, and two familiar faces approached the bookstore.

"Oh, there you are," Ginme called.

"Morning!" Kinme echoed.

The twin raven Tengu boys closed their red umbrellas and grinned at me. They stepped inside and immediately found chairs for themselves. It was clear they had business with me and not Shinonome.

"What brings you here? Looking for a book?" I asked.

The boys exchanged a meaningful glance, and Kinme ducked a hand into his pocket. I tensed, but Kinme merely produced an amanatsu orange. About twice the size of a winter tangerine, the fruit shone like the sun itself boiled and condensed down to this tiny treat. The refreshing scent tickled my nose.

"You see, Kaori reached out to us," Kinme said. "She was worried about you."

"We're good at finding lost things," Ginme said. "I mean, we can fly and have good eyes. Assuming there's good weather, of course."

I glanced outside. Though it'd eased a bit, the rain still beat down steadily. They'd get completely soaked if they tried to take off in this weather.

Kinme shrugged. "Basically, we're really of no use today. But I figured you must be bored too, right? So we came over to help you kill time."

Kinme split the orange in two, his nails tearing into the thin skin. The sweet and sour aroma of the fruit filled the room.

"Are you two stupid?" I asked. "I'm an exorcist. Leave me alone."

Exorcists and spirits were like hunters and their prey. The bloody, filth-choked chasm between us could not be crossed with mere fruit.

Or at least, that's how it should've been.

Ginme gobbled down a piece of fruit and cackled. "Yeah, we talked about this, didn't we? I don't mind. Besides, humans aren't the only ones who hunt spirits, so who cares? Anyway, this is pretty awesome. You should eat up."

How could they just overlook something like that? No matter how I tried to explain why we shouldn't get close, they just shrugged and insisted.

"Oh, by the way, apparently Tsuchigumo's gotten hungry," said Kinme. "It came down from the mountains and feasted on some of the Nue kids. Man, it's caused a real uproar. The Nue have all banded together and sworn to kill whoever was responsible. It's a mess, but bloody conflicts like this aren't actually all that uncommon."

"Are they that frequent?" I asked.

"Yup." Kinme popped another piece of fruit into his mouth. "I mean, who wouldn't get mad about someone harming people they care about? Humans and spirits are no different in that regard. Sure, there may be some spirits out there who have a grudge against humans at large, but most just want to live and let live. The kinds of spirits you hunted stepped outside those lines."

The light glinted coldly off Kinme's golden irises. "For example, if you did something to harm Kaori or Ginme I'd rip out those beautiful eyes of yours and feast on your bones."

Kinme seemed to loom up, even while smiling. His pupils narrowed. A chill emanated from his body, pushing away the humidity from the storm. An answering shiver tickled up my spine.

He was talking about killing me.

The back of my throat tingled as I recalled the days when I'd risked my life to fight spirits. The longer he stared, the thicker the tension in the room became. I held Kinme's gaze, all the while feeling as if a hand were squeezing my heart and lungs. Finally, I broke eye contact, but something nipped at my throat.

Then they both pounced.

The twins pulled me into a close embrace, chattering over each other in their excitement.

"Hey, no need to be scared!"

"It won't hurt at all, no worries!"

"That's not what I'm worried about!" I yelped, much louder than I expected. I cursed myself for falling for their little game, but they didn't let me wallow in self-loathing.

"Man, Suimei, that was great!" Ginme cheered.

"You've got perfect comedic timing," Kinme seconded.

Well, at least they seemed to be in a good mood today. They slapped at my shoulders, sometimes hitting places on my body that hadn't quite healed yet.

"Hey, cut it out, you idiots!" My yelling only made them laugh harder.

"Man, this kid is comedy gold." Ginme grinned.

"What the hell are you talking about?!" I howled.

The twins hugged their middles and nearly doubled over in laughter. I struggled to comprehend it all. Moments ago, they'd been talking about killing me; now they were laughing riotously. These huge, strong spirits treating me like their best friend had the power to break me any time they liked. Just what was going on here?

While I was getting more and more annoyed, Ginme wiped a tear away from his eye. "All right, all right, we're not gonna eat you. Of course we wouldn't. Maybe just a little taste is all."

"A little taste?!"

"Just a nip is fine, right? You'll hardly miss it," Kinme said.

"I'm pretty sure I would miss any part of me you decided to eat..."

Ginme cackled before mussing my hair. I slapped his hand away and fixed him with a glare, though he returned my gaze with a disarming smile.

"You, Noname, Kaori...everyone in the spirit realm seems oblivious to personal boundaries," I muttered.

The twins looked at one another and smirked.

"I mean, you're a fun guy. Of course we want to hang out with you," Ginme said.

"Besides, we need someone who can keep up with us in the teasing department," Kinme said. "Kaori just isn't able to follow along, you know?"

"Listen, I'm not your straight man," I said.

"But you are, aren't you?" Kinme asked.

I exhaled a sigh of profound annoyance. They'd barely been here five minutes and already I was exhausted.

From one breath to the next, I'd gone from terror to shock to annoyance—just way too many emotions in rapid succession. No matter how I tried to control myself, I struggled around Ginme and Kinme. And while no one here would criticize my *lack* of control, it still grated on me. What did it even matter out here, though? Even I knew it wasn't strictly necessary.

One of the best things about you, Master, is your sensitivity. My companion's voice rang in my mind. Whenever I failed and got locked away in the cell, he'd rubbed his soft body against me while saying those words. *They just don't really understand you, Master.*

I believed him. I'd caused all sorts of problems for the Shirai elders as they tried to teach me to rid myself of my emotions. Yet I smiled at the memory of my companion's gentle encouragement. Outside of my mother, he was the only one who'd ever praised or comforted me.

I blinked back to the present to find the twins smirking at me. "What?"

"Nooooothiiiiiiing," they said. And just like that, they snatched up their umbrellas and left.

"You really should smile more," Ginme called back over his shoulder.

"Later, Suimei," Kinme echoed.

After only a few steps, Ginme skidded to a stop. "Oh, I forgot." He returned and whispered in my ear, eyeing Kinme the whole time: "Do you...do you like Kaori?"

"Huh?" I was too stunned for words, but Ginme pressed on.

"I mean, she's cute and all, and I get that you'd be drawn to her," he said. "But I want you to know that I fell for her first, so don't get any ideas."

"What? No, wait..." The morning's headache attempted to

return. Why would I fall for such a childish woman who couldn't even act her age? "Spare me the jokes. There's nothing about her I find attractive."

Ginme cocked his head in complete confusion, but he smiled broadly all the same. "You idiot, she's an incredible woman. There's no one else like her."

"I just don't get you." I shook my head as I watched the twins leave. When I returned to the store, I noticed I was still holding half of the split amanatsu, so I nibbled on it. The juice burst in my mouth, delivering a perfect balance of sweetness and sourness as it melted away my fatigue, at least for the moment.

"I'm hooome!"

I must have lost track of time daydreaming because I hadn't anticipated Kaori's return at all. The moment she crossed the threshold, the glimmerflies that had followed her in a cluster scattered to escape the incense wafting through the house. Nyaa brushed past my leg on her way to the living room.

"I'll make lunch real quick, okay?" Kaori set down her shopping bag and made to head for the kitchen, but she froze the moment she looked outside.

I followed her gaze. The rain had stopped, and the clouds blanketing the sky had untangled. A puddle in the street reflected the strange colors of the constant night. Two small shadows interrupted the peaceful scene.

"Let's plaaaaaaay!" they sang.

The moment the rain let up, customers had arrived. Of course.

The two young children waited for us, giggling together under the clear sky. One, a little girl with long hair, wore a light-weight white yukata with a morning glory pattern of reds, blues and purples. The white fabric stood out sharply against the dark backdrop of the spirit realm.

Her companion was a boy with short-cropped hair. He wore a navy-blue yukata with a light blue belt. The contrast between his dark clothes and pale skin made him look as white as snow.

"Here it is! Here! I'm positive," the girl said.

"We want to read a book. Please loan us a book," the boy said.

The children spoke in a singsong before giggling and running into the store. Their wooden sandals with red threaded straps clacked on the road, the sound muffling when they stepped into a puddle. Their splashing disrupted the serenity of the sky reflected in the water.

Kaori shrank back. It was a strange reaction for her, considering she greeted nearly every spirit who visited with a warm smile.

I tilted my head in curiosity. "What is it, Kaori?"

Kaori hurriedly forced a smile. "Nothing. Anyway, we have customers. I need to get going."

She stepped forward to greet our new guests. Did I imagine that tremor in her hands?

Somewhere farther back in the store, Shinonome rolled over, muttering to himself. "Huh, is it that time already?"

With that, he passed out again, splayed out across the tatami flooring.

Just as I was about to demand some sort of explanation for all this, Kaori called out that lunch was ready. "Here you are, some mitarashi dango rice dumplings," she said. "Would you like one?"

"Thanks, lady!" the boy cried.

Kaori had purchased these dumplings, drenched in glossy, amber-colored sauce, as a snack. A special type of flour kept them from hardening even when cold, allowing you to soak them in the chilled sauce before eating them. With the rain ratcheting up the heat and humidity, a cool mitarashi dango really hit the spot.

"Mmm, yummy!" said the girl.

The boy and girl introduced themselves as Sasuke and Hatsu respectively. Each poked a dumpling with a toothpick, rolled it in the sauce, and took a bite. Their cheeks went pink the moment they chomped down.

"Mm, this is yummy, right, Hatsu?"

"I love it, Sasuke!"

"No worries, there's more," Kaori smiled at the children as they munched on their treats.

And yet... I couldn't quite put a finger on it, but something about Kaori was off. She looked no different from usual. Her complexion was pale, sure, but it always was—likely due to living in the spirit realm and having been away from the sun for so long.

However, even in the short time I'd known her, I'd never seen her quite so reserved. She tended to wear her emotions on her sleeve, which was perhaps why I had initially believed she was a high school student. To be honest, I still regarded her claims of being an adult with skepticism.

But she looked a bit more her age as she wiped at the children's sticky mouths. Now that I thought about it, she'd been looking after Goblin when we first met. Maybe she liked kids?

"She's an incredible woman. There's no one else like her."

Ginme's words echoed in my head. *Heh—I guess the way she takes care of people could be attractive if you saw her that way.*

I kept mulling this over until she turned and caught me staring. I froze. Her face reminded me exactly of one I'd seen before.

"Did you have one, Suimei?" she asked. "Noppera-bo's place only makes these for summer. They taste great when they're still chilled." The moment she mentioned the snacks, her face returned to its normal youthful exuberance. "Huh? What's wrong, Suimei?"

"Nothing. It's nothing."

She seemed to swap back and forth between childish and mature on a whim. Pretty impressive. I hid my concern by grabbing a dumpling. The aroma of the soy sauce mixed with the sweetness of the honey as I took a bite. I washed it all down with a sip of hot tea. Someone tugged on my sleeve. It was the little girl, Hatsu.

"Hey, do you still want that? You don't need it, right?" Hatsu was still munching away at her own dumpling as she stared at the one in front of me. Her plate was already clear. It was obvious what she wanted.

"Hey, um..." Pink tinged Hatsu's cheeks, almost as if she were embarrassed to even be asking. As she stood there entreating me,

I noticed for the first time the clear, insect-like wings that rested on her back. She puffed out her cheeks with impatience. "Can I have it?"

I sighed and offered up the plate. "You can have it."

"Thank you, Mister! You're great!" She kissed my cheek and, now armed with her spoils, made her way back to Sasuke's side.

"Eww, pretending to be precocious, huh?" he sniggered.

"Oh, shush," she sniffed.

These spirit children didn't seem to have a care in the world. I just focused on my tea to hide my annoyance.

"Thank yooooou!" they sang.

Once they were done eating, the boy pulled out something wrapped in a bamboo leaf. He undid the grass tie and set out the contents of the package atop the table. A small yellow stone. That was it.

"We'd like to pay with this," he said. "Will this get us a book?"

The stone, a chunk of amber resin that had been petrified many years ago, gleamed like fine champagne. The light reflecting within it from the glow of the glimmerflies turned it into a shimmering jewel.

Kaori brought it over to Shinonome, who held it up to his eye before offering an approving nod. Kaori turned to Sasuke and smiled. "Yes, this'll do. Please pick out what you'd like from our haunted bookstore!"

I cocked my head at Kaori again. Her slightly narrowed eyes, the raised corners of her mouth. Technically, it counted as a smile. But something about it was off, and I couldn't ignore it.

From that day on, things got busier at the bookstore.

Kaori mostly left the store in Shinonome's hands. For herself, she started using any available time between her shifts and her part-time job to go *somewhere* in the spirit realm. I wasn't sure exactly where. Plus, I was busy helping out at the store alongside Nyaa.

One day, I wrapped a book in a cloth and secured it to Nyaa. After that, we set out with Kaori, heading toward a small forest a ways outside of town. For a world of everlasting night, the forest felt bright. Something hung overhead in the sky, almost like the sun. It cast a strong light, illuminating the forest below.

I peered up. "Huh, so there are places like this even in the world of endless night?"

"This place is illuminated only in summer," Nyaa explained. "In autumn it reverts to dawn, and in winter it's covered in snow and darkness. Once spring rolls around, it's in a constant state of sunrise. This place is like a cradle for forest-dwelling spirits."

"What do you mean 'cradle'?"

"The people here change with the forest," Nyaa said. "It's a bit different from anywhere else in the spirit realm, where people tend to prefer stagnation or slow, calculated changes."

I didn't quite understand. Time worked strangely here, apparently. All I could do was listen and soak it in. It certainly felt like a real forest. Leaves scented the air, basking in the strange sunlight. The earth beneath our feet exhaled freshness with each step. The wind weaving between the trees caressed my cheek.

It was the closest I'd felt to a typical human summer since coming to the spirit realm. There were even cicadas buzzing in the distance. The forest brimmed with color and life, bright and vibrant and green.

"And we're here," Kaori said.

After a bit of a walk, we came across Hatsu and Sasuke's home.

The old hut sat wedged between towering trees. Time had stripped away the doors and much of the roof. The floor looked rotten. Was this place actually in livable condition? The interior certainly didn't appear lived *in*. Perhaps the children didn't actually stay here.

Kaori walked into the ramshackle hut, where the children greeted her.

"Hey, read us another book," Hatsu called.

"I can't read this kanji. Can you tell me what it means?" Sasuke asked.

"Sure, sure, but you two need to take turns," Kaori said.

"Okay!" the children chimed in unison.

Kaori patiently looked after them, almost like an older sister. In addition to the book they'd borrowed, they also had another that they wanted to read together. However, they struggled with the kanji and enlisted Kaori's help working through them.

"Read this one next. This one," Hatsu said.

"All right. Long, long ago..." Kaori started.

At first glance, they looked like great friends. Yet something churned in my chest—that uneasy feeling I'd had before. Kaori, flanked by the excited children, was smiling...yet she also wasn't. I searched for Nyaa. If anyone could read Kaori, it was her.

"What?" Nyaa grumbled. "It's hot out here, let's go in."

"I..." I froze before I even began. My elders and my mother shouted in my head not to get involved, not to let my emotions get the best of me. I dragged in several deep breaths before I finally steadied myself and shoved the screaming aside.

I had to know what was going on here. Kaori's smile wasn't right. It wasn't her. I couldn't stop thinking about how wrong it looked.

"Hey, cat. Why isn't Kaori smiling?" I choked out.

"Huh?" Nyaa's eyes flew wide with surprise. Then she sighed in resignation. "You're right, she's not smiling. I don't know much about human emotions and even less about their expressions—I'm just a cat, after all—but I can still tell. A gut instinct, if you will. Maybe I overlooked it because she isn't crying, like she used to as a kid. Pretty careless, I guess."

So there *was* more going on here.

The black cat pawed at the ground, pacing back and forth. All the while, she stared at me with her mismatched eyes, one gold and one sky-blue. "We met those kids about three days ago. Suimei, watch over Kaori for me. Maybe we missed it, but you didn't."

"What are you talking about?"

Nyaa's three tails flicked. "The height of summer is quite short."

The cicadas buzzed in sudden, abrasive unison.

In summer, with each passing day, the cicadas buzz louder and louder while the afternoon heat grows more and more intense. Although the rainy season had ended and the summer had begun in earnest even in the spirit realm, they didn't suffer the sweltering heat I was accustomed to in Tokyo—largely due to the simple fact that no sun hung in the spirits' sky.

That wasn't the case at Hatsu and Sasuke's forest home. Here, the sun beat down with a vengeance, the hot summer breeze whipped past our cheeks, and the high humidity pressed every last bead of sweat from our bodies. Reading books out here without the benefit of air-conditioning left us utterly exhausted.

At least Hatsu and Sasuke were enjoying themselves. They crowded around the book, craning to look closer every time Kaori flipped a page, talking excitedly about what was on it. Though they sometimes descended into squabbling, I couldn't help but be charmed.

"Amazing!" Sasuke crowed. "Being able to fly just with a fart?! I wonder if I can fly too."

Hatsu giggled. "I bet you can. Just eat a bunch of potatoes and you'll be blasting off."

"I'm gonna try it."

"Whoa, wait up, Sasuke," Kaori chided. "Keep your clothes on. You can't fly just by farting."

The children giggled as Kaori attempted to wrangle them.

"Hey, can you fly by farting, Uncle?" Sasuke asked, turning to me.

"No, I can't. And I'm not an uncle, either," I said.

"Huh. Boooooring," Sasuke sniffed.

"Besides, can't you fly with those wings on your back?" I asked.

"Oh! Right!" The children's laughter echoed through the ruined hut. At least they were in a good mood.

Yet all day long, Kaori's eerie not-smile never changed.

Eventually, even the rambunctious spirits ran out of steam and settled down for a nap. Kaori finally got a chance to rest as Nyaa laid a thin blanket over the sleeping children before curling up under it with them. Kaori sat back with more mitarashi dango that she had brought with us in a water bottle. We enjoyed them topped with a generous heap of ginger as she occasionally glanced fondly over at Hatsu and Sasuke.

"Thanks for joining me, both of you," Kaori said to me.

"It's nothing," I assured her. "I'm staying in your home, after all."

I sat next to Kaori with my share of the snack. The spiciness of the ginger clashed pleasantly with the sweetness of the sauce. Warmth spread through my body. We sat in comfortable silence only broken by the clink of ice and rustle of leaves. I'd never seen Kaori so quiet and sedate, but it was nice.

I set my empty cup on the ground and finally asked the question that had been burning in my mind all day. "So what happened?"

"Huh?" Kaori blinked several times. "You...you're surprisingly good at reading people."

"Surprisingly? That's kinda rude."

Kaori giggled and smiled as she looked at the sleeping children, patting their heads. She moved so gently, as though Hatsu and Sasuke could break at the slightest touch. "This is the first time I've seen them in ten years."

"Huh?" I cocked my head to the side. They hardly looked that old, maybe five or six max. If Kaori hadn't seen them in ten years, I guessed that meant they were some kind of spirit that didn't age.

"Hmm, how should I explain it?" Kaori pursed her lips. "You see, I first met Hatsu and Sasuke when I was a kid. Nyaa and I had come to the forest to play. It was summer at the time, and really, really hot, and the cicadas were so loud it was unbelievable."

I imagined Hatsu and Sasuke sitting there, all alone in the forest, when they spotted these newcomers tromping in to play. I could easily picture them inviting Kaori to join them.

"It felt like I had siblings." Kaori took on a wistful tone as she continued. "I didn't have any kids to play with at the time, since it was before Kinme and Ginme had taken on human forms. I was so happy to meet them. We lost track of time and played well into the night."

For the next few days, the four spent all their free time playing together. Once Hatsu and Sasuke learned that Kaori lived in the store, they asked her to lend them some books.

"They said that if they read a lot of books and memorized the stories, it might help take the edge off their boredom," Kaori said.

"What's that supposed to mean?" I said.

Kaori hesitated, staring off into the distance. However, her hand never once stopped stroking the sleeping children's hair. "I loved the time we spent together," she finally said. "We played a lot and read mountains of books. Every morning, I'd wait anxiously for them to arrive. Even though they were quite a bit younger than me, I was starved for friends."

A hot summer breeze passed through the hut, sending Kaori's hair fluttering about before sticking to her cheeks. Kaori tucked her hair back behind her ears and cast her gaze downward, her expression solemn. She suddenly looked much more mature than her age, her usual childlike wonder suppressed. It almost felt like she was giving up on something.

"One morning, after several days of rain, I was excited to see that the sun had finally come out," she said. "I took Nyaa with me to the hut to go play. That's when I found them, still and listless on the ground. I froze for a moment, mind reeling, before I screamed and ran over to them. The last thing they said to me was 'Thank you.'"

Kaori hugged herself, hands shaking. Her face drained of color as she stared off into the distance, almost as if she were reliving the memory as she spoke. "The moment they stopped breathing, a heavy weight fell on me. Right before my eyes, I watched as the heat left their bodies and their faces paled before finally turning brown."

"Kaori—" My voice came out harsher than I intended as I tried to stop her.

Kaori looked up, an indecipherable smile on her lips. "Ah, sorry..." She exhaled a deep breath and brushed her hand across Sasuke's cheek. "I didn't realize that these children were cicada spirits."

"Cicada? There are cicada spirits too?"

"Well, not everything you need to know is written in a book. These children have the spirits of cicadas, which means that they also suffer the same fate as cicadas." Kaori drew in a breath and let it out slowly. "As you know, cicadas have a short life span. Or, at least, it's short once they reach adulthood and crawl up out of the earth. But if they stay underground after climbing out of their eggs, they can live for years and years. They have surprisingly long lives for insects."

Suddenly, the buzzing of the cicadas stopped, as did the wind and the rustling of the leaves. It was an incredibly odd feeling to be surrounded by complete silence in the once busy forest. Deep down, a disconcerting feeling entered my heart, though I continued to focus on Kaori's story.

"These kids are a fragment of the dream shared by all the cicadas lurking underground, bored to tears as they bide their time," Kaori said. "Sasuke and Hatsu were born just like any other cicada, spending a long time in the soil before finally coming out of the ground. Once they reach the end of their lives, they die and are reborn, repeating the cycle over and over again."

A spirit that was locked in a continuous cycle of living, dying, and living again.

I swallowed and finally asked the question that had been on my mind for a while. "But...why?"

Kaori simply shook her head. "I don't know. One day, they were created, and that's it. Lots of spirits are like that. I mean, it's no easier a question to answer than why humans are born."

That made sense, at least. In a way, humans also existed in a cycle of life and death. I nodded and waited for her to continue.

Kaori's lip trembled with emotion. "Well, you know, we run a bookstore, and it's our job to bring books to those who want to read them. So, any time someone asks for one, I deliver it. If my job can help bring these children peace, then I'll gladly take it on with pride."

"Kaori..."

The closer you are to someone's death, the more it hurts you. To be honest, I didn't understand why she was putting herself through this again—her memory alone had made my chest ache. I didn't get it precisely because I had my own bitter memories of the agonies death brought. But in her own way, Kaori took pride in her work. I was an outsider to her life, and I really didn't have the right to object.

You must be strong. My mother's words echoed in my ears.

Kaori wiped at her tears and smiled that same awkward smile from earlier. "You know, it's funny, these kids have the same bodies and names as last time, but I don't think they remember me at all. Whenever I mention something that happened in the past, they don't seem to recall it. But I know it'll happen again. Our... separation."

Why was she making herself suffer like this? I didn't want to look at that odd, uncomfortable smile anymore.

"I'm an adult now," she said, "so I'm sure I can handle it much better than I did last time. I know this might cause some trouble for you, Suimei, but I'll do my best to make sure it doesn't."

I was cursing my own foolishness at this point. I'd thought Kaori was the same age as me. What had happened to the immature woman I'd first met? No. Kaori might have been a bit awkward, but she was more capable than most adults I'd ever met. She really was an incredible woman, one who could stand on her own two feet.

I really wished I could make her feel better. But how was I going to do that with my limited facility with people? And when

I could hardly understand my own feelings? How could someone younger, with less life experience, offer any comfort in a situation like this? My mother's sad expression flashed through my mind.

In my memory, I heard her words: *Any time you feel lonely, or like you might lose control of yourself, just pull Inugami close and sleep.*

I reached under the thin blanket that covered the resting children for the black cat napping beneath.

"Mreeeow?!"

I pressed the cat against Kaori's chest and looked straight at the wide-eyed woman sitting across from me. "You must be tired," I said. "Just hold her tight and take a rest. You'll feel better afterward."

"Where did that come from all of a sudden?" she said.

"Don't worry about that. I know you're pushing yourself. You need to take a break." I reached out and pinched Nyaa's nose as hard as I could as she continued to fuss.

"Hyaugh!"

"Hey, you're her friend, aren't you?" I asked. "Stop pretending you don't know what's going on and stick by her side."

"Gah! When did you get so violent?" Nyaa bared her fangs at me. Still, she turned in Kaori's arms, licked her cheek, and pressed her nose against Kaori's. "What do you need from me, Kaori?"

"Nyaa-san?"

"I'm not really good at thinking too deeply about things," Nyaa said. "As long as I can settle down for a nap in my favorite spot, that's all I need. You know that. So if you don't tell me what you want, I won't know."

Kaori smiled, really smiled, this time. "All right, then. Will you take a nap with me?"

"Sleeping is something I'm especially good at. Leave it to me."

"Great." Kaori rubbed her cheek against Nyaa's before lying down right there and closing her eyes. She pulled another light-weight blanket over herself. "There's a fan in my bag," she said, pointing.

"Wait, what?" I blinked.

"Hey, it's hot!" She smirked at me. Just like that, her usual mischievousness returned.

I shrugged, retrieved her fan from her bag, and dutifully fanned her.

"Perfect, just perfect." Kaori's eyes drooped closed. The cicadas resumed their chirping. The leaves stirred in the breeze, banishing that eerie silence. The wind was still hot, but somehow it felt lighter and less oppressive now.

At dusk, we all returned to the bookstore drenched in sweat, only to be greeted by an excited group waiting at the door.

"Hey, Kaori," Shinonome called, "Noname made her special cold nagashi somen today. Eat up!"

"We've got a special seat just for you—at the best place to get noodles!" Ginme said. "Come try our special cushions just for customers. Oh, and mentsuyu too!"

"What about our condiments? Personally, I'd recommend the ginger. Of course, cucumbers and chili oil are also available," Kinme chimed in.

"W-wait, what?" Kaori squeaked.

The three men hefted her up and carted her out to the back-yard, where they set her on the porch with a bowl of mentsuyu dipping sauce. It all happened in a blink, but Shinonome was already out there waiting for her with a vat of somen noodles. He grinned broadly and thumped his chest.

"I know you've been depressed lately," he said. "Anyway, you've always liked nagashi somen. Eat up and be merry."

"But why all of a sudden…?" Kaori cast her gaze down at the bowl of mentsuyu.

Shinonome patted her head before crouching down and looking Kaori straight in the eyes. "If you're having a tough time, just let me know. I'll take your place."

Kaori blinked a few times before bursting out in laughter. "Ah ha ha ha! No, it's okay. I decided to do this, after all, so I want to see it through."

"I see." When she nodded, Shinonome tightened up his sash and fastened his sleeves back. He let out a powerful yell and set a bamboo cylinder with the top carved away down in front of the vat. "All right then, let's eat up and put a smile back on that face. Ready? I'm sending the noodles down now!"

Ginme, sitting beside Kaori, had his chopsticks ready to go to grab the noodles that would slither down the length of bamboo. "Bring it!"

"Don't go eating Kaori's portion, Ginme," Shinonome warned. "I'll kick you right out."

"No worries! Probably."

"Gah, Kinme. Keep an eye on that idiot brother of yours."

Kaori snickered as she watched the men yell among themselves and excitedly joined the group. "Hurry up, Shinonome-san! I'm starving."

It was a relief to see Kaori back to her usual self.

Noname beckoned me over. "Hey, Suimei-chan. You get over here and join in too."

A cool, gentle breeze blew through the spirit realm, bringing a smile to my face as I slid on some sandals and headed over to join the others.

"Are you sure you're all right?" Noname asked.

Kaori nodded. "Yeah, I can do this."

"Hmm, all right." Noname handed her a packet. "This is incense. Be sure to add this into the fire. And that's—are you sure you don't want me to go?" Noname's mouth twisted with worry as she handed Kaori a bouquet of flowers.

Shinonome watched the exchange at a distance. Though he held a full pipe, he wasn't smoking at the moment, and his hand paused as he surveyed the scene.

"Really, this is fine," Kaori insisted. "Thank you, Noname."

Kaori took the large bouquet, smiled, and breathed deeply to enjoy the scent. Multiple layers of pure white chrysanthemums wet from the rain met her nose. Despite the rain, we had prepared to head for the forest again. Today was the day we would send off Hatsu and Sasuke.

Ten days had passed since we first met. The children had gradually grown weaker and weaker until they could no longer stand. Now, when we reached them, they lay prone in their futon, though Kaori never stopped reading to them. That was all they wanted. So, Kaori soldiered on, though she seemed more at peace with the process now.

"I'm going to wipe off some sweat, okay?" she said. "Do you need any water? No? Okay, I'm going to continue where we left off, then."

Kaori's soft voice filled the hut. She'd chosen a gentle story that day, but it had the children laughing as they lay there, which brought a smile to Kaori's face. As for me, I kept my distance and tried to hide my dark mood.

How strong she had to be to watch over these children with such compassion as they died before her eyes, when they looked just like her old friends. No, it wasn't strength. She'd struggled so much...until the day we ate nagashi somen in her backyard. Since then, she'd smiled more easily and sincerely, even on days when sadness lingered on her lips. What had changed?

A memory flashed in my mind—that of my mother hugging me and whispering that I needed to be strong. I swallowed down the pang that elicited and stepped forward to help Kaori.

The rain fell as fine as misty fog. The cicadas lay quiet around us. All that water made the verdant leaves more vibrant and drew a fresh, earthy scent out of the ground. The forest felt tense, still, like it was holding its breath in anticipation.

"Hey, Kaori..." Sasuke's voice was dry and distant. "Bring Hatsu to me."

Kaori and I shared a glance before I slid the girl's futon next to her brother's. Sasuke sighed in relief.

"We're a pair, you know, so we have to stay together 'til the end," he said.

"Sasuke..." Hatsu murmured.

"I'm so happy. Thank you."

Sweat poured down their foreheads, and their faces contorted in pain, though they still managed to smile at one another.

Kaori tried to draw their attention. "What should I read?"

Sasuke muttered a title. "'The Ants and the Grasshopper.'"

Kaori blinked with surprise before taking out a book. "Did you know that this story used to be about ants and cicadas?" she asked. "But as the story made its way to regions without cicadas, the grasshopper was used in its place."

"Really? I guess it fits us pretty well, then." Sasuke let out a long breath and closed his eyes.

For a moment, I thought it was over. However, upon closer inspection, I could see his chest still rising and falling faintly. Kaori's face tensed. Nyaa wound around her ankles and mewed. Kaori's expression softened as she stroked Nyaa. The cat settled in her lap as Kaori began to read "The Ants and the Grasshopper," one of Aesop's Fables.

While the ants worked hard during the summer months to store food, the grasshopper sang and played the violin, doing nothing to prepare for the harsh winter. When summer passed and winter arrived, the grasshopper found himself without any food. He asked the ants for help, but they replied, "You spent all summer singing, so perhaps you should spend the winter danc-ing," before driving him out. The grasshopper later died.

The story was often altered so the ants shared their food and the grasshopper played the violin in gratitude. In those versions, the ants and the grasshopper ate together in a warm room filled with laughter.

Once Kaori finished, Sasuke murmured, "Humans are pretty interesting." Then he shifted laboriously to face Hatsu, breaking out into a bright smile. "After a long period underground, we'll climb out again and dedicate ourselves to finding our companion. Right, Hatsu?"

She smiled back at her brother. "Well, Sasuke. I came out of the ground to meet you."

The two entwined their little hands and giggled.

Kaori and I exchanged glances. Just what were they talking about?

Sasuke closed his eyes and continued, voice gentle. "I'm sure the story is calling all of us spirits destined to die at the end of summer lazy. Grasshoppers, us. I guess people think that way. But we're so desperate to leave something for the next generation that we don't have time to think about ourselves."

"Humans live far longer than we do," Hatsu agreed. "Surviving the winter is an important ordeal. But we don't have to worry about it. All we have to concern ourselves with is living summer to the fullest. Don't you agree, Sasuke?"

Sasuke lowered his eyes and laughed wryly.

Sweat ran down their foreheads. Kaori grabbed a towel and

wiped it away. Sasuke smiled and thanked her as he stared up at nothing.

"Back in the old days," he said, "I didn't need anything other than summer. I figured there was no use in knowing about anything beyond that. But it was *boring*. I was tired of simply waiting in the soil for that one summer to come. And then we met you, Kaori. You read us books and told us about all the other seasons. Through your stories, you showed us a different world. After that first summer, I enjoyed a completely new life before it all went pitch-black again. Even when we return to the soil, we'll never get bored."

Sasuke let out a long breath and closed his eyes. Hatsu gazed lovingly over at her brother and reached a quivering hand toward Kaori. Kaori squeezed the tiny hand, leaning close to hear each softly spoken word. "Kaori..." Hatsu whispered.

"Yes?"

"Thank you so much. Thank you for expanding our world. Thank you for sticking with us, even though it must have been painful for you. Like I said last time, I'm glad to have made such a kind friend."

Last time?

Kaori's eyes flew wide. A tear slipped out, trailing down her cheek. "You didn't forget?"

"Of course not."

More tears flowed from Kaori's wide eyes, dripping off her chin.

"We spirits can connect feelings," Hatsu said. "I don't remember everything from the past, but I'll never forget what's important. I love you. All the feelings and memories of that love are still in my heart and my brother's. Whenever we invited you to come out and play, you always smiled so brightly. I remember playing tag and splashing in the river. And, of course, reading a lot of books."

Hatsu fell into a coughing fit and Kaori rubbed her back. She was pale by the time it subsided. "Kaori..."

"It's okay," Kaori said. "I understand. You don't need to talk anymore."

But Hatsu pushed on anyway in a voice that was little more than a wheezy rasp. "I'm sorry...for making you cry again."

"Hatsu..." Sasuke, his eyes still closed, hugged his sister and whispered in her ear. "I'll take over." He smiled up at Kaori. "I can already see the dream."

"Hm?" Kaori leaned in.

"Down in the soil, we'll dream of the books you read us," Sasuke said. "When the earth grows cold, we'll know it's winter. When it gets warm, we'll know it's spring. When it gets heavy with fallen leaves, that means it's autumn. We'll dream of playing in the forest in every season. And we won't forget the taste of the mitarashi dango we ate together. We'll also remember Suimei. These dreams will play through our minds over and over until the summer when we're meant to awaken finally returns." Sasuke looked up at Kaori. "When that day comes...do you want to play?"

Kaori clenched her jaw and nodded. Tears streaked down her cheeks and her nose ran. "Of course I do, my dear, dear friends."

Sasuke's eyes drooped closed. He smiled. "I didn't have a chance to tell you last time, but this isn't goodbye. My...our memory will pass on forever, and we'll cross paths with you again. We just have a bit of a ways to go...so...so..." A tear rolled down his cheek.

"Let's meet again," Kaori promised.

The forest boomed as cicadas buzzed in unison. Outside the hut, the rain stopped and the sun burst through the canopy of trees.

"Sasuke? Hatsu?" Kaori murmured.

Sasuke and Hatsu were holding each other's hands and smiling, as though they had just passed into a peaceful sleep. Sasuke's last words lingered in the air, a promise that they would all meet again.

Nyaa helped dig a hole where we could lay Sasuke and Hatsu side by side in the earth. Kaori placed white chrysanthemum flowers atop the little graves while I burned the incense Noname had given us. Kaori stared at the ground with empty, dry eyes depleted of tears. I bowed my head and put my hands together in prayer.

"They'll be back, you know," Nyaa said. "Ten years is practically no time at all."

Kaori didn't respond.

"These things in the ground are mere shells of who they were," Nyaa said. "There's nothing important here, nothing to be sad about."

Kaori just kept staring at the ground. Some strange feeling overtook me, and I walked abruptly over to her.

I faced Kaori straight on. She stood slightly taller than me, a fact I tried to ignore. Were I a bit older, this would have looked a lot cooler. I pulled Kaori into a rough embrace.

"Wha...?" Kaori stiffened, though she didn't resist as I held her against me.

My heart pounded, my face burned, and my hands trembled uncontrollably. I could only hope that Kaori didn't notice, though none of that mattered right now. I cleared my throat.

"Ten years is a long time, I know, even if it might seem like nothing to these spirits. Maybe these bodies *are* just shells, but to you, they were your friends, and ones that were important to you. There's nothing wrong with being sad, with feeling lonely, with feeling pain at saying goodbye. Even if you know they're coming back, it's not that easy to let go. Spirits just can't understand these things." I squeezed her tightly and spoke into her ear. "Just let go and cry...dummy."

Humans should be allowed to feel sad. Not that I, a person forced to suppress his own emotions, was in much of a position to say such things. I mumbled an apology and backed off. Maybe I had gotten through to her. Maybe I hadn't. Hopefully someone around her could help.

Kaori quivered. "Is it really okay?"

What a stupid thing to ask. I wrapped her up in another impetuous hug and told her to do whatever felt best. She threw her arms around me and let out a wail. Around us, the cicadas still sang. The sun still beat down. The remnants of the rain still glistened on the leaves.

The forest echoed with the song of the cicadas, reverberating through the forest all summer long.

Deep down in the soil, curled up like a baby in the womb, we started to dream.

In our dreams, a little girl ran under the summer sun in a glimmering forest. She teased her feline companion before turning around and smiling innocently. "See you tomorrow! We'll always be friends, okay?"

The girl waved until she was well out of sight. She faded away behind a curtain of rain. When the girl reappeared, she was crying.

The cicadas buzzed on.

The scene shifted, bringing a new summer.

Beneath the brilliant sunlight, the girl, now older, read a book to us. She stroked through my hair, sending a tingle down my spine. Hatsu and I requested more stories, and the girl shook her head and laughed, and then she indulged us until our day arrived and we had to depart.

Plish. Plosh.

Summer came again. Wooden sandals clacked as we approached the bookstore. A woman inspected our faces from behind the open door. She hugged us tightly around her protruding stomach.

Yet another summer came. We found an unknown child at the bookstore this time. When I asked if they wanted to play, they smiled, the expression oddly familiar.

Time passed. Like bubbles on a pond, more days floated by, disappearing as they popped. That once crying child was now completely calm. Though I loved her formerly plump and child-like hands, her thin, wrinkled hands felt just as nice in my hair.

Aaah...

A stream of light pierced the cold, dark earth as yet another summer arrived.

Another year where we could spend a whole new summer together with our friend.

CHAPTER 3

Memories of the White Clover

THE LAMPS ARRANGED around the store cast a dim, yellow light throughout the cluttered interior. It felt like an old family home, something built many generations ago with all sorts of Japanese-style knickknacks filling up the limited space. Everything from trinkets to sundries to lamps lined with traditional Japanese paper, old antique dressers, and framed Japanese paintings piled high.

The general store maintained a quiet, peaceful presence in the back alleys of Kappabashi, located in the Taito Ward in Tokyo. Founded generations ago, the place was known for serving both regular customers and wholesale partners alike.

I was setting out the latest products while customers chatted excitedly as they browsed the shop. During this time of year, fireworks festivals were held every weekend. That drove up demand for small accessories to accompany summer kimono and yukata.

As I worked, a man approached. "Doin' good, Kaori-kun."

"Why, thank you."

The man's name was Toochika, and he was the owner of the store.

Despite the summer heat, Toochika-san wore a brand-name suit and leather gloves with his hat pulled down low. Between his clothing and his mustache, he looked like a fashionable older gentleman. He waved me over and presented me with a book. "Can I leave this with you?"

"Of course. But I have to say I'm a bit surprised. You usually like to bring it back yourself and enjoy a drink with Shinonome-san while you two get into it over something or other."

Toochika-san shrugged and slid his hat to the side, revealing the white plate riddled with fine cracks that was the top of his head. "This heat has really gotten to me lately. I'm thinking of going to the river for a while to take a break and meet with some friends I haven't seen in a while. Unfortunately, that means I don't have time to go to the spirit realm. Please give my regards to Shinonome-san."

Toochika-san was a kappa spirit—an old one at that—from right here in Kappabashi.

I'd originally thought the name of the area had something to do with the legend of the kappa, but Toochika-san laughed that off. Perhaps he'd been here for a long time, maybe even longer than the bridge itself. Now he worked as a merchant selling a large variety of products in addition to running a general store. In fact, Toochika-san also served as a wholesaler for home appliances in the spirit realm. He was one of a number of spirits who lived among humans. Some even held political office.

Though humans would never guess it, the boundary between the human world and the spirit realm was quite blurry.

"Leave it to me," I said. "I'll tell Shinonome-san."

Toochika-san nodded and gazed down at the book before he let out a long, hot sigh. "I have to say, you have a wonderful bookstore. There's no way I could have gotten my hands on that book without you. I had such a great time, I couldn't put it down for a whole week."

Toochika-san put his hands to his chest as if basking in the afterglow of the experience.

We carried quite a few books that had been lost to the human world or that were otherwise rare and difficult to obtain. That made the store something of a paradise to booklovers like Toochika-san. However, we rented these books out at such high prices that they rarely circulated.

"Oh, and thanks for letting me take some time off on such short notice," I said with a bow.

Toochika-san waved it off. "No worries. Spirits are quite active in the summer months, and I imagine your shop must be as well. It's really no big deal. Besides, you're Shinonome's precious little girl, so how could I refuse?"

"Little—hey! Don't treat me like a kid."

Toochika-san chuckled at my objection. "It seems like just yesterday that you were still so small. But my apologies, I'll keep my jokes to myself. Anyway, thanks for showing up to cover for the worker who called out, Kaori-kun. You're a lifesaver."

"No worries. I'm just happy to have a job."

Toochika-san winked. "You're quite humble, one of your many adorable traits."

Suddenly, I heard a yelp behind me. When I glanced over my shoulder, I saw a gaggle of female customers both young and old going red in the face. Toochika-san waved at them, and another shriek spiked through the shop. Kappa spirit or not, the owner of the shop was quite popular among this brand of customer, who thought of him as rather cool and fashionable.

"Oh, by the way..." Toochika-san took something out of his chest pocket. "Here, I found this sandwiched between the pages of the book I borrowed. Does it belong to a customer?"

He held out a bookmark made of traditional Japanese paper, crafted by hand with flowers pressed into it. Judging by the rough edges and uneven texture, it looked as it if had been made by an amateur. It had clearly seen a lot of use, judging by the wear and tear.

I took it with a frown. "Hmm, could be. Maybe it belonged to the last person who borrowed that book."

"Possibly," Toochika-san said. "Anyway, I must be going. It looks like the afternoon worker finally showed up, so I guess you're just doing the morning shift today. Leave the rest to her and go home early. If you're late, that idiot father of yours will lose his mind."

"I, uh...okay."

"Be careful on the way home." With that, Toochika-san made a gallant exit.

I inspected the bookmark in my hand. It was an average little thing, with four-leaf clovers and white clover flowers pressed into it. For some reason, I found myself intrigued.

Upon returning to the spirit realm, I set about my cleaning for the day, trying to keep my face blank. After a break for lunch, I returned to my task, still maintaining that cold expression.

"Hey, Kaori. Kaori!" Shinonome-san called. He followed me around the house like a baby duckling trailing after its mother. He kept peering at my face, trying to read my expression, though all he really managed to do was get in my way.

I finally broke. "Gaaah! What?! You're so annoying!"

"A-annoying...?!" His jaw dropped. "I'm just worried about you is all."

"Why? Can't you see I'm fine?"

He muttered something under his breath and scratched the side of his head. "Well, umm, you know, I heard that you cried about that thing that happened the other day, and well, I thought maybe you were lonely, so..."

"Huh? It's fine, nothing for you to worry about."

Shinonome-san slumped his shoulders in defeat, voice weak. "Well, if you say so."

To be fair, he wasn't wrong about the crying. Taking care of Hatsu and Sasuke as they grew weaker and weaker had nearly torn my heart apart. I'd desperately tried to stay calm even while struggling for soothing words to say to my dying friends. I'd been scared, so very scared, and there had been absolutely nothing I could do about it. I'd just told myself that it was my job and I had to do my best.

With the support of my family and friends, I managed to see it through. Still, even knowing that Hatsu and Sasuke would be reborn and we'd meet again, I hated to watch my friends wither away like that. I broke down in the end. I knew I should've sent them off with a smile, but I hadn't been able to help it.

These things in the ground are mere shells of who they were, Nyaa-san had said at the time. *There's nothing important here, nothing to be sad about.*

As someone who had lived in the spirit realm, it made sense for Nyaa-san to feel that way. However, it did little to calm the emotional turmoil swirling inside me.

And then...

There's nothing wrong with being sad, with feeling lonely, with feeling pain at saying goodbye. When Suimei spoke those words, the taut threads of sadness straining within me finally snapped.

However, I had apparently cried a little too much, because even just hearing about the event had sent Shinonome-san into overprotective parent mode, which was actually quite annoying.

I sighed and pinched Shinonome-san's cheek.

"Eyach...hey!" he wailed.

"You worry too much, you no-good codger," I said.

"Can I really be all that bad if I'm worried about you?" Nonetheless, he finally eased up.

I placed my fist over his heart. "I never said there was anything wrong with worrying, did I? Just don't overdo it."

"Hmph." Shinonome-san scowled, the first time I'd seen his expression change since I got home.

Just then, Suimei came into the living room. "Hey, I want to head out soon."

Right. I'd promised to accompany him on his search for whatever he was looking for.

I packed up the cleaning supplies. "I'm going out with Suimei," I said to Shinonome-san. "Please keep watch over the store...and try to calm down."

"Kaori..." He frowned.

"See you! Come on, Nyaa-san, you're coming too."

"Mreow?!"

I scooped up my best friend, who was right in the middle of her nap, and hurried out of the bookstore. Before we left, I remembered that odd bookmark and grabbed it as well. Couldn't hurt to have that with us while we looked for—whatever we were looking for.

Speaking of which... "You're searching for a spirit, right?" I asked Suimei. "Do you have any leads?"

"No. Nothing in particular," Suimei admitted.

"Hmm, I see." I raised the book, with the bookmark nestled within, and smiled. "Well then, maybe you can join me in what I'm looking for too."

Suimei blinked several times before finally nodding in agreement.

Glimmerflies fluttered in their lamps, illuminating the streets of the town. We encountered more traffic than usual traversing the main street. Spirits tended to be more active in summer. Something to do with souls getting restless, according to Shinonome-san. I wasn't entirely convinced by this claim, but true enough, summer brought all sorts of out-of-towners to market.

Consequently, merchants kicked into high gear, which just added to the crowd. A glut of food stalls lined the street, filling the air with all sorts of delicious scents. Other shops sold bizarre souvenirs and trinkets. All the merchants shouted, trying to attract more attention. The lively mood would linger until Obon—the festival of the dead—when the spirits would return to their native homes.

"Hey, ma'am, can I have one?" I said to a merchant. She offered an array of bright red candy apples at a stall beside the road. The glimmerflies' glow reflected dully off the bright, sugar-coated surfaces.

I bought two and offered one to Suimei. He shot me a stern look. "I don't need one."

"Too bad, you've got one."

I persisted until he accepted the candy. I already knew he liked sweets; it was too late to defend his masculine sensibilities.

I chomped on the apple, and sweetness and acidity warred in my mouth. My cheeks relaxed with pleasure. A glance at Suimei revealed he was enjoying his as well, if in small, reserved bites.

"You know, I never thanked you," I said—a bit of a non sequitur, I know.

Suimei tilted his head in confusion as he took another bite. I wondered if he even grasped how much he'd done for me.

I struggled to verbalize just what that simple hug the other day had meant to me. Were it not for him, I'd probably still be bawling my eyes out. Not only that, the act had revealed a softer side to Suimei. A happier side. I didn't know if that was great news for him, considering the demands of his family business, but...he seemed less tense, less worried, less jumpy about being in the spirit realm.

I smiled and plucked off a piece of caramel clinging to the side of his lips. His eyes went wide as I pushed it into his mouth. "Thank you for helping me back there," I said.

He flushed bright red. "Are you crazy?"

"Hey, now you're getting mad at me? I was thanking you."

Suimei stumbled back and jabbed a finger at me. "Are you still so oblivious? You shouldn't be doing things like that with members of the opposite sex."

"But you said that I always acted like a child, didn't you? So who cares if someone as childish as me does something like that, huh?"

"Don't make me keep repeating myself! You're a full-fledged adult."

"Hm?" Well, it seemed Suimei finally saw me as a grown woman. It was rare to hear him say that, considering how he often treated me like a child. It was certainly an improvement, but it was also kind of embarrassing. I mean... "F-fine, I'll be careful."

"That came out odd," he muttered. "Just forget I said anything."

We both stood there, our faces burning. It felt like every spirit passing on that crowded street gawked at us. Was that why I felt so warm?

"What are you looking for, anyway?" Suimei grumbled.

"Oh, that's right." I presented the bookmark again. "I'm looking for the owner of this."

Toochika-san had selected quite the rare book to borrow. Only a handful of spirits had borrowed it over the last couple of years, all of them regulars, and only they could have left the bookmark behind.

"I figured it was a good opportunity to catch up with people while searching for the owner of this bookmark," I explained.

"Catch up?"

"Yes. You know, thank them for their patronage...and..." I stumbled. I needed to choose my words carefully so I didn't inadvertently make Suimei angry—I had this nagging fear that for some reason he might reject me outright. I braced myself before continuing. "And...introduce you," I said. "See, I think if you say hello to everyone, they might help you find what you're looking for."

Suimei's eyes narrowed, face closing up. "I'm an exorcist."

"That's fine. It doesn't matter."

"What makes you so confident?"

"I said it's fine, didn't I?"

Suimei fell silent.

"I know what I'm talking about," I insisted. "So please, believe me."

No matter what I said, I couldn't seem to reach him. Then his shoulders slumped in defeat.

I understood his reluctance. Though Suimei had lost his powers, he was still an exorcist. Some spirits didn't mind, but plenty would never come around to trusting him. But a lot of our regulars held respectable positions in the spirit realm, so they would no doubt be of great help to him, if we could earn their cooperation.

Cicadas buzzed, jolting me back into the moment. My chest tightened around the familiar sound, but then the memory of Suimei's words seeped into my heart, soothing the ache. I treasured those words as much as I treasured anything. As such, I was more determined than ever to help him find what he was looking for—though I didn't want to force the issue.

"I'm sorry," I said. "You don't need to come if you don't want to."

Suimei said nothing to that.

"Let's go. We're almost there." I regained my composure and started walking.

As we headed east, I greeted acquaintances that we passed in the street. Thanks to the festival, glimmerflies glowed in red lanterns hung along the streets, turning the town bright and beautiful, a truly one-of-a-kind experience.

"Kaori." Nyaa-san nudged my shin. "He's gone."

"Huh?" I stopped short, whirling around. Sure enough, Suimei was nowhere to be seen. I rushed to retrace my steps, fearing some spirit had attacked him, only to find him standing calmly a little ways off. Relief washed through me.

Suimei was staring intently at his surroundings. It was quite the scene. Long row houses filled this area, like you might see in a historical drama. Lively spirits occupied these buildings, far different from the quieter residents near the bookstore. A Tofu Boy carried his wares on a long balancing pole over his shoulders. A glimmerfly seller walked by to peddle his wares. An Ittan-Momen hung himself out to dry with the rest of the laundry. Several women stood around a well, making small talk as their children played about their knees.

"C'mere, Taro!" a child called.

"Aroof! Ruff ruff!" Suimei very nearly smiled as an excited puppy bound toward the child who had called for him. It looked like the puppy was what had caught Suimei's attention. He almost seemed to be smiling at the sight of this innocent play, though there was also something lonely in his gaze.

"Do you like dogs?" I asked him.

"Not particularly... But he's just like the spirit I'm looking for, Inugami. He's slightly longer than a dog, with black and red spots. The long head and pointed ears make some people think he looks like a weasel. He's the real reason I came here. You see, he was my partner. We worked together as exorcists."

"Wow." I blinked. "But what made you tell me this all of a sudden?" Until now, he'd never said anything about the spirit he was searching for other than that he was looking for it.

Suimei thought it over for a moment. Then he bowed his head and faced me. "I want you to introduce me to your customers. I understand if you prefer not to because I'm an exorcist, and

I know there's not much I can do to repay anyone, but...I want to find my partner as soon as possible. He's...like a part of me."

A part of him, huh? I wondered if that meant this Inugami was used as a weapon in exorcisms. Or maybe it was more than that? Suimei's blank expression revealed little.

"Leave it to me," I thumped my fist against my chest. "I'm going to repay the debt I owe you. On my spirit honor."

"Debt?"

I snickered and thrust my hand out at him. "If you don't know, that's fine. I'm glad you helped me, so thanks!"

Suimei wore a complicated frown, but he eventually held out his hand. Just as we sealed our pact, Nyaa-san shouted at us to get moving.

"Hey, it's really hot out here!" she called. "Let's get this out of the way so we can hurry on home." She lay on the side of the road, glaring at us.

Though a lot more pleasant than the human world, we could still work up a sweat here. Suimei and I quickly headed to our destination: A room in one of the many row houses around us.

We stepped through an ordinary door into an ordinary room just off the street. Or it would have been ordinary except for the sign reading Umbrella Repair. Beyond the paper-covered screen doors awaited a world of red. Bright vermilion paper covered Japanese-style umbrellas with complex skeletal frames. The finished models lined up against the wall were truly works of art.

The light from the glimmerfly lantern in the corner cast crimson shadows across the walls, dyeing everything scarlet. A warm mixture of glue, oil, paper, and fresh bamboo scented the space. The moment we stepped inside, the noise of the streets hushed to a whisper.

The owner of this shop was, of course, an umbrella-related spirit known by most as the Ghost Umbrella, One Leg, or even the Ghost Karakasa. I just called him Karakasa-niisan. He wore a stylish black kimono and an umbrella atop his head, though the oil paper of his umbrella was yellowing and torn in places.

He looked through one of the holes in the umbrella and eyed the bookmark before shaking his head. "Hmm, no idea," he apologized.

"That's all right," I said. "Sorry to bother you."

"No, not at all. Oh, just wait there." He limped into the back room, laughing as he searched for something. Eventually, he returned with a wooden box. He sat on a tatami mat and cracked his neck. "Sorry. I haven't heard much lately. I've been rather busy because of that kappa."

Naturally, Toochika-san was the kappa he was referring to. Toochika-san also purchased goods from the spirit realm. It was often the only place to get certain handcrafted goods humans had stopped producing. With the recent boom in popularity for traditional Japanese crafts, Karakasa-niisan was earning a healthy profit from his sales to Toochika-san.

"It's good to have some money to live on, which also affords me the time to read to my heart's content and catch up on books," Karakasa-niisan said. "None of that was possible when I was a human. I've never been happier."

Karakasa-niisan pulled a bowl of glue over. As a human, Karakasa-niisan had been a broke, masterless samurai who did umbrella repairs just to make ends meet. Even then he'd loved reading, though. His desire to read had not diminished as a spirit, and after many twists and turns, he had ultimately become one of our regulars.

He offered me the wooden box. "You said you wanted to eat this the other day."

Confused, I opened the box. I gaped at what I found: Red bean paste sandwiched in a thin, pale yellow wafer crust. This was monaka, a famed snack made by Noppera-bo! Sold seasonally and only in limited quantities, it was so popular that you couldn't buy it unless you lined up well before the store opened. Moreover, I couldn't justify the high cost—it was even more expensive than normal monaka.

I involuntarily swallowed as Karakasa-niisan nudged the box toward me again. "You can have it, if you like," he said. "I'm not a fan of sweets."

"Are you sure?"

"Of course." He smiled warmly between the gaps in the umbrella. "You're always such a great help, Kaori."

"Thank you!"

"If you find the spirit your friend is looking for, please let me know. Oh, one more thing..." Karakasa-niisan offered me a large piece of cloth dyed a brilliant dark blue, meant for carrying items while traveling. "Take this. You're going to all the other regulars, right?"

"Oh, thank you. But why are you giving this to me?"

Karakasa-niisan just grinned. "You'll understand in due time."

Thanking him again, we left the shop and made our way to the other regulars.

Umi Zato lived in a fisherman's hut right on the beach.

"Oh, well, hello there, it's great to see you," he said when we approached. "Hmm? I'm afraid I don't know anything about the bookmark. Hey now, I've got some dried fish right here, do have some. As much as you can carry. Inugami? I don't know anything about an Inugami, but I'll look for it. Hey, have some mollusk. I've got some top-grade shellfish right here just for you, and they're huge too."

He grabbed a whole bunch of dried fish and mollusks from the back of the hut and pushed them into our arms before bellowing out a laugh, the wrinkles in his face creasing even deeper than usual.

"No worries, no worries," he said. "You used to play with me in the sea when I was just a wee lad. There I was, standing out there gazing at the waves and you came over to befriend me. I'm eternally grateful."

Umi Zato gently stroked my head. I smiled at the memory.

When I was little, I had always played with Umi Zato when I came to the seaside. We would use shells to make little houses. That had been a long time ago, though, and I was surprised he still remembered it.

"Hmm? You want more dried fish? Shellfish?" he asked.

"No, no, that's quite enough. Thank you!" I carefully put away the items he gave us and bowed deeply to hide the tears stinging my eyes.

"Come stop by again sometime. I'm always here." Umi Zato saw us off with a strum of his lute.

Everywhere else we traveled that day, we left with more souvenirs. Everyone welcomed me in as soon as they saw my face. It seemed Karakasa-niisan had anticipated that—hence the cloth. By the time we reached the last of the regulars, gifts and trinkets filled the bundle.

"Well, it looks like you've got quite the haul there," Noname said. Yup. That's right. Noname was the last of the regulars. She had also borrowed the book in question, but unfortunately she knew no more about the bookmark than anyone else we'd talked to that day.

"Then whose bookmark is it?" I mumbled to myself as I sipped the cold jasmine tea Noname had brewed for us.

"I'm sure you want to go home soon, don't you?" Noname said. "Did you introduce Suimei to everyone? How did it go? Did they agree to help?"

"Yeah, it went okay. Everyone told me to let them know if I find Inugami."

"Well, that's good. I wonder if they'll call Suimei a Strangeling soon as well."

"Ah, I hope so. Then he'll be able to go out alone." I glanced over at Suimei. "What's wrong?"

His mouth had returned to that old complicated frown. "Why are all these spirits so quick to help me? I just don't get it. No one seems worried that I'm an exorcist at all."

"They said they'd help, so who cares about that?"

"No, it's not that. It's...gah, I feel like I'm going crazy here. Just what are spirits anyway? All the ones I ever exorcised didn't care for humans at all. It's just weird seeing them trying to help me out. Is there something wrong with them?"

"Isn't it hard to live your life doubting everything?" I asked.

"I'm only suspicious of spirits," he muttered, disgruntled. "I'm still an exorcist, after all."

Noname smiled. "I suppose it's only natural that you'd feel that way. Just like humans, there are many kinds of spirits out there. But you know, their fondness for humans is only a recent development—at least for the ones around Kaori."

My eyes widened. "No way!"

Noname smiled. "What's so surprising?"

"No, I mean...it wasn't always that way? This is new?"

Noname snickered. "All this change is thanks to you, Strangeling."

Strangeling...that was what the residents of the spirit realm sometimes called me. I frowned. "Huh...I always thought 'Strangeling' was a word for a human who had settled in the spirit realm. Is that not quite true?"

"'Strangeling' can refer to a human being from the outside—from the human world," Noname confirmed. "But it also refers to a human being who has blown a breath of fresh air into our restricted world. There have been several others in the past...but now it refers specifically to you, Kaori."

"What? But what did I do?"

"Don't rush me," Noname chided. "Try to listen through to the end first. Anyway, we spirits are generally quite lonely."

"Lonely?"

"Hmm, how to put this? I don't mean that we're alone. We live together in a large town like this, after all, just like humans who built villages to live together. However, we don't interfere with one another."

This I understood. I'd seen it happen. Even if a stranger's neighbor disappeared or an acquaintance dropped dead in the street, spirits might feel nothing and pretend it hadn't even happened. Suimei's brow was creased, and he nodded with interest.

Glancing at him, Noname pointed at me. "This child, the Strangeling, changed everything. I wonder if anyone has told you, Suimei—she was a real crybaby when she was younger."

"Kinme mentioned it," Suimei said. "But what's your point?"

"Thanks to Shinonome-san's tireless efforts, she cried less and less over the years. In fact, whenever she saw a spirit, she would do everything she could to get close to them, no matter how dangerous. Let me tell you, it was pretty rough parenting her at that age."

I shuddered at the thought of a toddler stumbling over to an immense, menacing spirit. What had I put my adoptive parents through back then?

"Spirits, unlike humans, have incredibly short childhoods," Noname went on. "I guess we're like animals in that sense. People here aren't used to dealing with infants. We didn't intuitively realize that if you take your eyes off them, they can easily end up endangered. They can fall, cry—all sorts of bad things. If you leave them alone, they'll die."

"Die is a bit extreme, don't you think?" Suimei winced.

"It isn't! What if they're walking down the road and fall into a gutter? Or they jump out in front of a running spirit? Or slip in the bath? Or swallow a toy? Human mothers are amazing. I truly respect them. When Kaori arrived, we quickly learned we couldn't just leave her to her own devices and keep to ourselves. We had to change."

Oh, dear, I'd been a real terror as a child, hadn't I? Noname continued, describing how any time I howled "Let's play!" the spirit realm quaked. Once I got a hold of someone, I would conscript them into playing with me for hours on end. And the glowering bookstore proprietor was always fast on my heels to keep me safe. Were something bad to happen to me...well, let's just say spirits feared to see me hurt while he was watching.

"Everyone was reluctant at first, but before you knew it, they were looking forward to hearing the sound of your little footsteps." Noname chuckled. "We became comfortable with your warmth and learned we could hug you without hesitation. We came to cherish this human child and her bright, innocent smiles."

Noname rested her chin in her hands and smiled gently. "I didn't even realize how lonely I felt until you came along, Kaori. I learned the joy of hearing someone's laughter and the warmth of thinking about another person. Everyone began to care about you, and the whole atmosphere of the spirit realm grew livelier."

Noname's beautiful amber eyes fixed on mine as she stared deep into my soul. I couldn't help but relax under her lovely gaze.

"Previous Strangelings had also brought great change to the spirit realm," she said. "You, Kaori, changed the minds and hearts of the spirits who live here. Wouldn't you agree, Nyaa?"

Nyaa-san thumped her tails against the floor. "I still have a strong memory of those days. Everyone was extremely over-protective of Kaori. And of course, we also received a lot of gifts. So anything Kaori asks of me, I'll do it without hesitation...even if it's related to an exorcist."

I squirmed under all this attention, staring down into the glass in my hand.

Noname stroked my head, so gentle and motherly. "The regulars at that store were the first to fall for Kaori. I think of you like my own child, though perhaps I spoiled you a bit much. You're still quite childish for your age."

"If you realize that, you could just start treating me like an adult, you know," I said.

Noname wrapped her arms around my shoulders and laughed. The sweet, floral scent of her perfume filled my nose, leaving me feeling shy, almost like I wanted to cry. More than anything, I really wanted to avoid that.

"No matter how much I may want to treat you like an adult, that's quite a challenge in its own right," Noname apologized. "From my point of view, your arrival was still just a short time ago, and I can hardly keep up with your growth. Most spirits live far longer than humans. Plus, the flow of time is different for us. Maybe that's not an excuse, but please forgive me if I still spoil you a bit. Anyway, I think I've rambled on quite enough."

"Huh?"

"You're looking for the owner of this, aren't you?" Noname said, pointing at the bookmark. "Well, I'll tell you where you can find them."

Noname sent me off with a mischievous wink.

Noname's information brought us to the Nasu Highlands.

Off in the distance stood Mount Chausu, one of the primary peaks of the Nasu mountain range. Vast grasslands and shrubs filled a region devoid of any buildings or signs of human life. Only birdsong and the rustling of the wind filled the air. Unlike the hot and humid haze that swirled around Tokyo, a pleasant breeze blew across the plateau. In the distance, cows grazed. White clover grew all around us, their three leaves swaying in the breeze as they basked in the sun. Pretty white flowers poked out between the leaves.

After having passed through hell, this seemed like heaven. Nyaa-san, Suimei, and I paused for a rest, and I made my way to the lone tree growing in the meadow. There I found Shinonome-san, dressed in his usual yukata, lazing about underneath the tree with his pipe in his mouth.

"Hey, what about the store?" I asked as I sat beside him.

"I left a customer in charge," he said.

"What?"

"He's a regular." He waved his hand. "I'm sure it's fine."

Some customers were more than happy to mind the store since it meant they could read to their heart's content. That was probably what had happened today. I still couldn't believe how cavalier Shinonome-san was about it. No way could you get away with that kind of thing in the human world.

"You're just slacking off," I scolded.

Shinonome-san narrowed his blue-gray eyes and pouted like a child. "Oh, shut up, you." He sighed, reaching over to ruffle my hair.

I could understand the allure of playing hooky in a place like this. For a while, we just enjoyed each other's company in the shade of the tree in the meadow. It practically glowed beneath the dazzling summer sun.

"You used to bring me here a long time ago," I said.

"That's because humans need to be exposed to the sun."

That was true enough. Shinonome-san had understood when I was a child that humans could get sick without sunlight, and thus he'd taken me to the human world every so often. Many times, we'd come here.

"I would chase Nyaa-san around and eat the lunch Noname prepared for us," I remembered. "It was a lot of fun."

Shinonome-san looked just the same now as he had back then, thanks to his being a spirit with a long life span. As he lay there smoking his pipe, I was transported to my childhood. I'd changed so much, but him, not at all.

"I'm sorry about earlier," I said. "Did I hurt your feelings?"

Before we left, Noname had informed me that Shinonome-san

came by to complain to her about my remark earlier in the day, when I called him annoying. He merely shook his head with a wry smile. That left me relieved.

I reached into my bag, finally digging out the object that had brought us here in the first place. "Is this bookmark yours?"

Shinonome-san blinked and swiped it from my hand. His ears burned a bright red. "I was looking for this. Thank you."

"Well, I'm glad I found it! But what is it? It's pretty old. You don't seem like the type to be messing around with pressed flowers, either, so I didn't put it together until Noname tipped me off. I ran all around town looking for the owner."

"Aah...hmm." Shinonome-san shifted and took a long drag on his pipe. Several moments passed before he let out the white smoke and watched it waft away into the sky. "The...the flowers in this bookmark, well, you gave them to me the first time I brought you here. I couldn't bear to throw them away, but I didn't know what to do with them. Noname suggested I make a bookmark, and, well, I did."

"You made this?" I gasped.

"Fine, yes, it was me! I did it all. I originally thought about asking some craftsman to make it, but that jerk Noname seemed to enjoy making me do it." He scratched at the back of his head and refused to make eye contact.

So these were white and four-leaf clovers that I'd picked for him? Though I remembered coming here, I had no recollection of giving him flowers. Still, I could easily imagine it, considering how many white clovers blanketed the hillsides. It made sense that I'd spent time searching for four-leaf clovers, making crowns out of intertwined flowers, and all that.

And Shinonome-san had kept my first little offering all this time. This, coming from the same bumbling old man who couldn't even do his own laundry.

In a fit of emotion, I smacked Shinonome-san on the back. I didn't know what to say. A simple thank you didn't seem right, but neither did a joke. But wow, I couldn't believe what a sweet old softie my adoptive father really was.

Shinonome-san desperately tried to evade my hand, crying out that I was being too rough.

"Damn that Noname for telling you it was me," he grumbled. "Who does she think she is? Here I am trying my best to look like a cool, strict father."

Shinonome-san continued to mutter about his ruined image as I sat there blinking. Finally, I broke out laughing, the sound carrying across the empty meadow. Shinonome-san frowned, concerned, but I couldn't stop laughing. I was just so happy that he thought so much of me and tried to be a good father.

"Aaah, my sides hurt from laughing so hard." I rubbed at my sides as Shinonome-san stared off into the distance with an affronted look. I shifted over to sit closer to him and placed my head on his shoulder. "Don't be silly. I think you're cool... and I know that I can always rely on you. I'm proud to call you my father."

He swallowed hard. Glancing up, I saw the flush in his face, but I pretended not to notice.

"Hey, you're proud of me too, aren't you?" I asked.

"Of course! You're the heart and soul of the spirit realm."

"I think that's going a bit overboard!"

"Hardly. That's a fair evaluation, I'd say."

Hey, Shinonome-san... Though I couldn't voice the words, I spoke them in my heart: *I wonder if I'll always be your little girl, even when I become an old lady. Will you treat me any differently then?*

Of course, I could never bring myself to actually ask this. Shinonome-san was a spirit, and a very long-lived one at that. I was just a human with a relatively short life. Time moved at very different speeds for us.

Suddenly, I remembered Sasuke and Hatsu and cast my gaze downward. One of these days, I too would die, and I was sure Shinonome-san would be quite saddened by it. Still, I didn't want to leave his side. This man who had watched over me from such a young age was immensely important to me. I loved him. I never wanted to make him sad. But I knew that he would one day suffer if we remained close.

I tried to sound more cheerful than I felt. "Well, if you say so, I guess I'll just have to go with it. I'll do my best to keep being a daughter you can brag about to others."

"I guess I'll do the same, then," he agreed.

"Great, then I want you to wake up every morning before me, shave that awful stubble off your face, and actually eat your lunch. Oh, and wear some proper clothes for once! You've gotta take care of yourself."

"Ack! Where'd that come from?"

I held Shinonome-san's gaze, even as he scowled at me. "You said you wanted to be a cool father, didn't you?"

Shinonome-san averted his eyes, though he mumbled out a promise to give it a shot.

I smiled and turned my attention back to the meadow. It seemed like such a strange place, considering the hustle and bustle that surrounded us every day in the spirit town. Deep in my heart, I hoped that we could return to this place soon. In ten years, twenty years...as long as time would allow.

"Hey, wait a minute," Suimei shouted. "Get that thing away from me."

"Kaori! Shinonome! Look at this! It's amazing!" Nyaa-san called. She was bounding about with a giant rat held tightly in her teeth.

Goosebumps spread over my skin, and I reeled back. Shinonome-san went pale and sat up straighter.

"Hey, I got a nice meal," Nyaa-san crowed. "You should be congratulating me."

"Wow, uh, that's amazing, Nyaa-san," I stammered.

She giggled. "Aah, it's been a long time since I caught such a fine specimen. Here, I'll show you."

"No, that's okay, you can have it all to yourself! Please don't bring it any closer!"

With that, the serene moment between Shinonome-san and I shattered, and we were pulled back into the chaos of our normal lives.

Laughter Bubbling Up from the Sea Floor

T HE SUN NEVER ROSE in the spirit realm. Once the lights went out, thick, oppressive darkness blanketed the town. During those hours, nothing, not even private residences, gave off any light. Not even the moon could pierce that inky veil.

The lonely hollows of the trees, shadows cast by stones, puddles, old and decaying wells...these were the places from which countless eyes gazed out at the world. Though they stayed out of sight, they were so numerous you could feel their presence tickling the back of your neck.

If you listened carefully, you could even hear the sound of someone breathing right next to you. The moment you let your guard down, these spirits would pounce and scoop out your entrails.

That was the world of the spirit realm, the underbelly of the human world, the darkness lurking beneath the light. The true world.

Off near the river, just outside the town limits and away from the faint shine of lights, a glow shimmered on the surface of the water.

One spirit was doing his best to escape the heat.

Nue was a strange spirit, sporting the head of a monkey, the limbs of a tiger, and a snake for a tail. In the west, many would have called him a chimera. According to legend, this was the sort of spirit that Minamoto no Yorimasa had slain. Now, he slid his incredibly long tongue out between his fangs to drink from the river and eat a stolen peach.

Spirits were generally pretty good at tolerating the summer heat, but it was particularly miserable today. Nue, who usually lived with the rest of his pack in the much cooler mountains, had come down to experience the liveliness of summer in town, but he had quickly come to regret it.

His family had given him a little money as a farewell gift, but he'd lost it all when a talented merchant talked him into making an exorbitant purchase. In return, he'd received a delicacy un-like anything he'd tasted back home. Still, it lacked that special something human flesh offered. And now he had to sleep outside, which theoretically he didn't mind, but his wallet was so empty that he could afford no measure of comfort at all.

Maybe he should have just stayed cooped up in his home village after all. He had only come down here in the first place because of his desire to kill Tsuchigumo, the monster who had slain several Nue children. He shouldn't have stayed.

Nue sighed deeply and gazed up at the moon. Somewhere

back home, his friends and family were looking at this very same moon, but he couldn't reach them. He cried out, his howl echoing on the empty wind. Usually, he heard howls in response from his kith and kin. Now, there was no one around to hear him.

When his loneliness drew his head back down, he found a silver thread had entwined around his front legs. The thread, whiter than the light cast by the moon, extended from the water's edge to Nue's legs.

He tilted his head and tried to untie it. As soon as he touched the thread, something yanked, dragging him toward the river like a fish on a line.

"Augh!" he screamed.

Nue tried to resist, digging his feet into the ground, but more threads burst from the water to wrap around him, covering his entire body in the silver thread. Whatever was pulling him dragged until his toes dipped into the mud at the river's edge. A tingle shot up his spine at the touch of the cold water as he screamed with all his might.

"No, stop! If you kill me, my clan will have their revenge! They'll chase you to the ends of the earth, tear out your intestines, and cast you into the bowels of hell just like we did with Tsuchigumo!"

Of course, this was all a front. No one back in the village would know about his death out here, and so they would do nothing about it.

Right when he figured it was all over for him, the force pulling him into the water weakened. At the same time, an unfamiliar voice rang in his ears.

"Did you kill the spider? Hmm, well, that's gonna be a hassle." The voice somehow combined the boisterous snarl of an older woman and the sultry murmur of a younger one. Undercutting it all was the distinct bite of annoyance. "Oh, so you all joined together to kill it? Smart move, smart move..." she mused.

The silver thread began to unravel and draw back into the water. As soon as he could, Nue screamed wildly and scrambled away from the water's edge.

Soon, all that remained were the sounds of leaves rustling, insects chirping, and a woman's sigh.

"Stupid spirits," she said. "They flock together just like humans do. I really hate being chased down like that in the name of revenge. Now, I wonder, is there a stray still hanging around somewhere? Tee hee hee..."

A fish splashed up out of the water, and an instant later, the woman's voice faded away, along with any trace of what she had done.

CHAPTER 4

The Lady of Kashikobuchi

THE FLAMES ROARED.

Even from this distance, the heat burned my skin, as though I stood in the flames that punished sinners in hell. Someone reached out for me, their face contorted with agony. When I was young, I had wanted to help at times like these—they had looked so pained, so pitiful. But Shinonome-san told me these souls were atoning for their sins and that a new life awaited them once they had done so.

"This way, even if you make a mistake, you can make good on it eventually," he said. "It's nice to know that there's always a way to find forgiveness."

I knew he was right, but I spoke up anyway. "Isn't it awful that you can't find forgiveness until after you die? Why not forgive someone when they're still alive? Is this really salvation?"

"Then why not look at it this way? Whenever you think that you can't forgive someone, or whenever you learn that someone is worried over not being able to forgive another, consider how you can attain that forgiveness. There's no need to forgive everyone, of course. You can forgive them when you can or find another resolution when possible. As long as you keep that in mind, I think that at least a few more people will be able to reach the salvation they need."

"Hmm, Inugami?" The red oni looked thoughtful. "Can't say he's been seen around here."

"I see..." Suimei's expression grew heavy, and he turned for the exit.

It'd already been a few weeks since we started looking for Suimei's partner. Recently, he'd been searching every day, scouring the spirit realm, even calling upon our old acquaintances, but all to no avail. Maybe Inugami wasn't in the spirit realm at all.

I shook my head to banish the thought. I couldn't say that to Suimei, not with how hard he was looking.

"I'm going to the beach next," he said. "He hates water, so I don't think we'll find him there, but let's give it a shot anyway."

"I understand, but...don't you think you should rest a bit?" I asked.

"Sorry, but I don't have that kind of time right now." Dark circles hung under Suimei's eyes. He hurried to the next location, refusing to rest even after days and days of frustration.

"Dammit..." he muttered.

I couldn't stand watching him biting his thumb in frustration.

I wanted to help somehow, but the whole situation dragged on no matter what we tried.

We finally arrived at the door connecting hell and the spirit realm. When I pushed, the old door creaked in protest, but it opened. The air of the spirit realm, especially cool after traversing the fires of hell, sent goosebumps rippling over my skin.

The familiar sights of the spirit realm greeted us. It seemed it must have rained while we were gone because the ground was wet and a fresh scent rose from the damp earth.

"Huh?"

Someone was waiting for us. As I looked closer, I realized it was Kinme, soaked through by the gentle rain.

"What's wrong?!" I asked, rushing over.

"You can't go anywhere else today," he said shortly. "Go home."

"What do you mean?"

"Just listen, okay?!"

I stammered an apology, completely taken aback. Kinme was always so calm... What could have riled him up like this?

Suimei stepped past me and yanked Kinme close by his collar. "You know I'm running out of time. If you want me to go home, you better explain."

Kinme glared at Suimei for a moment before his anger softened into pain. "Ginme was attacked."

"Ouch, ouch! Cut it out, Noname!"

"Be patient. And stop moving!"

Ginme thrashed as Noname attempted to tend to him.

We'd rushed back to the bookstore after Kinme's dire pronouncement but found things mostly under control by the time we got there. It looked like Noname was taking care of Ginme and he'd be fine.

"Welcome back, you two. Did you get caught in the rain?" Ginme wore a massive grin, as though nothing at all had happened.

"I came back because I heard you were attacked!" I gestured at his injuries.

"Hmm? Oh, that's right. I'm a bit absentminded right now." He scratched at his head before showing us the bandage on his neck.

He had been assaulted while he was off on his own, visiting a friend in the human world. Just as he opened the door in the spirit realm to take a shortcut through hell, someone had jumped him.

"Suddenly, a strange thread unspooled from the darkness. Before I knew what was happening, my neck was wrapped up tight!"

"Could you possibly be any more careless?" Kinme scolded. "We're always telling you to be careful, especially in the summer when all these new spirits come to town."

"I get it, I get it. I let my guard down right when I was going through the door."

"Well, don't!"

Ginme cackled at his indignant brother.

Kinme grabbed Ginme by the collar and snarled at him. "Try to be a little more reliable," Kinme snapped. "What would I do if you were gone? You're my only brother."

Ginme gently stroked his twin's head and despite himself, Kinme deflated.

"Listen, I'm sorry. I won't let my guard down anymore," Ginme assured him.

"You better promise me, you idiot."

"It's a promise."

Shinonome-san, who was smoking his pipe in the corner of the room, watched this tender display with wide eyes. For once, Kinme got to be comforted by his suddenly mature brother.

"It looks like some hooligan crept in during the hustle and bustle of summer," Noname said as she started cleaning her tools. "A number of children have been attacked in the past few days by a spirit who uses thread to carry away their victims. They strike from the darkness and try to drag the victim off somewhere. I wonder if it plans on eating them..."

"You mean like a predator?" I asked.

Noname shrugged. "They do seem pretty hungry. A lot of spirits come to town around this time of year. I guess it's not that surprising."

"Yes, but...do you think everyone will be okay?"

Plenty of the spirits in town were more or less powerless. I feared any of them becoming this creature's next target.

"They're okay," Noname assured me. "This person seems to only target spirits who are alone."

Ginme nodded. "Yeah. I was attacked when I was alone. As long as the weaker spirits stick together, they'll be fine."

"In that case, I guess it'll be okay..."

"I've issued a notice to the townspeople not to go out alone," Noname explained. "That should limit the damage this fiend can do."

I was relieved to hear measures had already been taken. Once summer ended, the number of people in town would drop almost overnight and whatever spirit was out there would probably wander away. It seemed like a long wait at the moment, though.

However, while I'd relaxed, Suimei was clenching his fists, his face even whiter than usual as he stared at the floor. What was up? Just as I was about to say something, Suimei stomped toward the front door.

"Where are you going?!" I grabbed his shoulder to stop him. It was too dangerous for him to walk around alone under normal circumstances. And now?

Suimei pushed me aside and muttered in a low, angry voice, "I'm going to look for him."

"Where?! We still don't have any clues!"

"You think I don't know that?" His hands trembled as he brought them to his face. "I have a bad feeling. I need to find him as soon as possible. If he's here in the spirit realm, he'll certainly be alone."

All the blood drained from my face. But I couldn't let him go by himself. "If you're that worried, that's even worse. You need to stay calm."

"Let me go. I'm going to bring the fight to them!"

"It'll do Inugami no good if something bad happens to you. Let's gather some information first. We'll go around to the people

I introduced you to again. Many of the people here operate at their own speed, so they could have easily seen Inugami and forgotten to contact you."

"Do you really think we have the time to leisurely stroll through town?!" He glared, hazel eyes bright, but I had to keep my cool.

"Please, listen to me. I'm sure the spirits will help you."

"Do you really trust them?"

"Huh?" For a moment, I had no idea what Suimei was saying. I wanted to believe I'd misheard him, but the incensed look on his face said different.

"Can you trust spirits?" he repeated.

"Stop it..."

"They're all spirits at the end of the day. Even if they pretend to be good people, they're ultimately after flesh and blood. Is there any guarantee that they haven't eaten my partner? Can you say with any certainty that they aren't all laughing at me as I search this town?!"

"Stop it!" I threw my hands over my ears and stared hard at the ground instead of at him. Suimei's words swirled in my head. Sure, there were a number spirits who had a taste for flesh. Some even ate live prey like animals, but—

But they weren't the only spirits out there!

I jerked my head back up and grabbed Suimei's arm. We stared straight into each other's eyes, and I clenched my jaw, refusing to back down from his glare.

Finally, his gaze wavered.

I took a deep breath. "You've spent a long time as an exorcist.

It's what you spent most of your life doing. So it's understandable that your experiences taught you not to trust spirits. After all, exorcists and spirits are natural enemies. You don't even think about it. However, much like you, I've lived most of my life in one context—in the spirit realm. Spirits have watched over me since I was little, even at times being overprotective. So yes, I can say this with confidence: They will help you."

Everyone was watching our back and forth in silence.

Please, everyone, trust me and leave Suimei to me. I smiled, just a little. "Give them some credit. Remember all the time you've spent here. Has anyone lied to you? If you still can't find it in your heart to trust them, then trust me, the 'human.' I believe in the spirits here, and I'd never betray you. I promise."

Tears slipped out as the rush of emotion overwhelmed me. Suimei had only spent a short amount of time with the spirits. However, I truly hoped that would had been enough to warm his heart.

The tension in Suimei's body eased. The next time he spoke, his voice hardly rose above a bashful whisper. "I'm sorry. I kinda let the stress get the best of me."

"Well, then..."

"I believe you. Thinking about it, that's the only reason why I'd still be here."

"Exactly!" I was so overjoyed that I pulled Suimei into a tight embrace.

"Hey, wait, stop it!" He yelped in surprise and tried to tear himself away, but I was taller and easily held him against me.

Someone cleared their throat behind us.

"Ah, uh, Noname?" I smiled bashfully.

"Well, well, it looks like things are nicely wrapped up here," she said. "Anyway, don't overdo it or your father might get jealous."

I quickly released Suimei and caught a glimpse of Shinonome-san glaring. I'd never seen an expression quite like that on him. I stepped away from Suimei and smoothed down my clothes. I hadn't done anything wrong, yet I still somehow felt guilty.

"Meeow." Nyaa-san curled around my feet. I scooped her up in an attempt to hide my embarrassment.

"Customers are here," Nyaa-san said.

I rushed to open the sliding door connecting our home to the store. "H-hi," I greeted them. "Oh, it's been a while."

Standing there in the shop were none other than Goblin and Yamajiji of Oboke. Goblin shuffled shyly from foot to foot.

"Uh, so..." Goblin said. "We heard you might need our help."

"Don't lose sight of me. There are a lot of dangerous spirits living out here," Nyaa-san said.

"All right, got it," I promised.

We followed Nyaa-san through the hovels located on the outskirts of town. She was currently the size of a tiger and had flames licking around her feet as she kept a keen eye on her surroundings.

This area was home to spirits who couldn't settle in the town proper. Of course, due to the nature of the area, it wasn't exactly the safest. However, everyone, even the more hostile spirits, ducked out of the way at the sight of Nyaa-san.

"Kuro! Kuro, where are you?!" Suimei yelled, heedless of the stares he drew. He was truly desperate to find his companion.

Goblin and Yamajiji had given us the information that led us to this place. After hearing that the family living in the bookstore was looking for Inugami, they came all the way out here to tell us about their sighting.

"It's really a pretty small detail, but I hope it helps," Goblin had said. "I recently saw an unfamiliar spirit who looked pretty beat up. Maybe you should check it out?"

The news left us all stunned. Goblin's sources were Karakasa-niisan and Toochika-san. It seemed they'd used their network to spread the word about the missing Inugami. The fact that word had even reached Yamajiji, who usually lived deep in the mountains and rarely came to town, said a great deal about how far the story had traveled.

Suimei had taken in the information with a blank expression, then bowed and thanked them. I could only hope that this helped change his perception of spirits.

I scanned the decrepit buildings around us. A familiar face appeared at the corner of my eye.

"Nene-san!" I said, rushing over.

"Oh, Kaori-chan! It's been a long time. How have you been?" Nene-san wore a simple teal short-sleeved kosode with her sash tied at her stomach rather than her back. Underneath her hood, powder covered her face. She had neither eyes nor a nose, just a blank face.

"Well, I'm looking for a spirit," I said. "Actually, I'm searching for one that looks like a dog, but with a longer body and covered in black and red spots. Have you seen him?"

"Hmm, I've heard rumors of a spirit like that lately..." Nene-san's mouth, the sole feature on her face, curved upward in a smile, baring her black-stained teeth. "Come to think of it, I think I saw it just a little while ago, stumbling around on the road opposite this one. Maybe you should go check."

"Thank you!"

I bowed my head to Nene-san, one of the Ohaguro-Bettari spirits known for their stained black teeth, before taking Suimei's hand.

Nene-san called after us as we ran. "I'll let everyone know, okay? If you get lost, just stop a spirit and ask for help!"

"Thank you, Nene-san!"

"Anything for my sweet Kaori-chan."

I waved over my shoulder as I continued to dash in the direction she'd indicated. Smoke curled up from the homes lining the street as dinnertime neared. I called out to each spirit I found to keep us on the right path, but when we reached the area of the sighting, we stopped short in a dead-end alley.

Then it started to rain again.

The lukewarm summer rain drenched us, but we no longer cared. The sight that lay before us was too shocking for us to worry about such things. The neglected alley was cloaked in darkness. It was so remote that even the glow of the streetlights didn't reach it. Even in the gloom, I could make out the blood painting the walls and ground.

"No!" Suimei's face went white and he dropped to his knees.

The coppery scent of blood hit me. It dripped down the walls and pooled on the ground. Black hair littered the scene. Deep gouges rent the earth in places. Whatever had happened here, it was clear it had involved a fierce battle.

I took a few steps back, nauseated from the smell of blood.

Just then, I saw something stuck in the fence of a nearby house: a silver thread smeared with bright red blood. The torn thread swayed in the wind.

"That's spider silk," I said. "And...hmm, what's that?"

Nyaa-san tilted her head and sniffed the silver thread. "It smells like calligraphy ink."

Suimei remained on his knees, staring blankly at the ground, at the trail where something had been dragged away.

We followed the trail of blood on the ground, but it quickly tapered off as the rain washed it away. Suimei was increasingly frantic, desperate to believe the blood wasn't Kuro's. I asked the nearby spirits for information, but they had seen neither the spirit who was responsible for this nor Inugami. We were at an impasse.

"Where could they have gone?" I frowned.

"It's too soon to give up," Suimei insisted. "There's...there's got to be something we can do."

First, we had to figure out just what kind of spirit we were dealing with here. Nyaa-san and I put together all the information we'd gathered. First, we knew they attacked in darkness and only when a spirit was alone. We had also found silver thread smeared with blood and a trail indicating the victim had been dragged away.

"The culprit must be a spider spirit," I concluded.

Nyaa-san nodded. "I agree."

"They're also the type who would use thread to catch their prey. But even when they catch something, they take it back to their home rather than eating it right there on the spot. We need to find their nest."

What spider spirits did I know of? Tsuchigumo, Jorogumo, Ogumo... Which one hurt Kuro?

Left with no other leads, we headed back to the store. Perhaps Noname or Shinonome-san knew something that could build on these new clues.

As soon as we got back, we passed through the store and into the main building, where Noname and Shinonome-san waited with grave expressions.

"Hey, what's wrong?" I asked worriedly.

Shinonome-san wore a grim look as he offered me a book. It was the first volume of Toriyama Sekien's—*The Illustrated Demon Horde's Night Parade*. "We've got trouble," he said.

"Huh?"

"After you left, a customer came to return this book. Then he mentioned something strange. Some of the pages are blank."

I flipped through the book and, just as Shinonome-san said, some pages were totally blank. Where there should have been a picture and name, now there was nothing. I started reading from the last remaining passage.

"A type of Tsukumogami, Jorogumo: A shape-shifting spider spirit that can take the form of an attractive woman. This spirit believes it is truly the thing it has taken the form of and, in some cases, may eat people."

Another entry. As I read it, my blood ran cold.

"Tsukumogami: First introduced in the *Tsukumogami Emaki* scrolls drawn in the Muromachi period, these are items that have become spirits over the course of one hundred years, and they find joy in deceiving the hearts of man. They are known collectively as Tsukumogami."

Suimei scowled. "What does this have to do with Kuro?"

"In ancient Japan, it was believed that things that had been around for a long time gained mysterious powers. Some of our books are more than one hundred years old, and they're also considered Tsukumogami."

"I don't get it."

"Every year, I do a thorough cleaning to ensure that no Tsukumogami are born, but...I guess I wasn't thorough enough last year." I turned to Suimei with a stricken expression. "I'm so sorry. This is all my fault."

We cleaned the many antiques in our home once a year as a

measure against Tsukumogami. How could this have happened? I didn't know how to apologize properly for having caused so much trouble.

Suimei shook his head. "Don't worry. The Tsukumogami is the one who decided to attack Kuro, not you. It wasn't your fault. It wasn't anyone's fault." He was trying to sound calm, but I could tell his voice was shot through with anxiety.

When we went out to search for the Tsukumogami, the sun had set on the human world, its light little more than a faint reminder off in the western sky. We stood watch on the banks of the Hirose River, a popular landmark in the city of Sendai, located in Miyagi Prefecture. This was the largest tributary of the Natori River, famous for the ayu fish that swam upstream through the city.

Untamed nature surrounded us. The river sat lower than usual thanks to construction farther upstream at the Okurakura Dam—streets evolve with the times, and so do rivers. Our hiding place was situated beside Kashikobuchi, one of the many deep pools along the river's course. These tranquil pools, which ran deep and calm, provided an ideal environment for fish...and many more mysterious creatures.

For ages, people had spoken of the terrifying things that lurked in the depths of these bright yet ominous blue-green pools. Rumor and folklore abounded. Naturally, Kashikobuchi had its own specific legends.

According to one, a man had gone fishing when a spider suddenly wrapped a thread around his leg. The man removed the thread from his ankle and secured it to the root of a nearby willow tree. A moment later, he heard a powerful roar, and the willow tree was dragged straight into the abyss. The man stood there, stunned, as the spider said: "How clever..."

That was how this place had come by its name—it literally translated to "clever abyss."

"Are they really going to come here?" I asked.

Shinonome-san nodded. "There was a door leading to Hariyama Hell in the area where Inugami was last seen. This shortcut leads to Tohoku, which makes the Kashikobuchi Jorogumo a sure bet. Besides, we found a black hair at the shortcut's exit. I'm positive." He set a hand on Suimei's shoulder. "Don't worry, we'll get your companion back. I intend to take full responsibility for what my book has done."

Suimei stared at Kashikobuchi, his eyes fixed on the silver thread spanning the river. It was almost beautiful as it caught and reflected the dim moonlight.

Nyaa-san suddenly popped out of a bush. "Noname, Kinme, and Ginme are waiting on the other side of the river. I also asked a spirit who lives nearby, and he said that the spirit who inhabited this place died a long time ago. That thread was definitely made by a Tsukumogami. That means we're in the right place."

"Hmm, so that means that the Tsukumogami probably also thinks that she's the true spirit of this spot. A fake pretending to be the real thing... What an awful spirit, harming Suimei's friend like that."

Shinonome-san's eyes narrowed as he examined the water, foot tapping. While I understood his anger, I'd rarely seen such rage in the eyes of my easy-going father. A mere glimpse of his exposed teeth as he growled sent an unfamiliar surge of fear through me.

"A fake will never be the real thing, and I'll make sure she knows that," he snarled.

A chill ran down my spine. I hated it.

"Shinonome-san, don't forget why we're here." I strained to keep my voice flat and even.

He finally regarded me, a wry smile smoothing away some of the anger. "I know. We're here to get Suimei's partner back. You don't need to remind me." He shrugged and stared off into the distance. "What I'd give for a smoke..."

I sighed with relief. Now that was more like the man I knew.

We settled down to wait. There was little else we could do at the moment.

Despite the light from the nearby homes, the riverside was cloaked in darkness. Everything past a certain distance disappeared into the gloom. Not exactly the ideal environment for waiting for a spider known to eat humans.

"How much longer, do you think?" I whispered over to Suimei in an attempt to lessen my anxiety. "I bet you're looking forward to being reunited with Kuro."

A deep look of sadness washed over his face. "Honestly, I'm not really sure."

"Huh?" Surprise made me speak louder than I intended. "What do you mean?"

"I'm still not sure if it's really okay for me to see him again."

"But you were so fixated on finding him just to be reunited again, weren't you?"

He shook his head and gazed out at the lights from the homes on the other side of the river. "Hey, Kaori, could you forgive someone who ate your parents?"

"What?" I sat there, mute. I was too shocked to even process what he'd said. I attempted to speak, but...but I just couldn't get the words out.

Suddenly, I was suffocating as something bit into my neck, instantly blocking the blood flow to my brain. The world around me dimmed to black. I struggled in vain to remove the thing from my neck, but the world only grew darker.

"Kaori!"

Hot air blasted against my cheeks, singing my skin as Nyaa-san burnt away whatever was tied around me. I coughed and gagged as I heaved in fresh air.

"Are you okay?!" Nyaa-san asked.

I gasped for breath. "Haah...yeah...I'm fine."

Through my tear-streaked vision, I picked out the remains of something still burning: a sticky, silver thread emitting a dull glow.

As soon as I realized what I was looking at, something heavy dropped onto my back.

"Aww, the sweet fragrance of a young girl."

The voice seemed to belong to a woman—one who was pressing me down into the riverbank. Drops of cold water poured off her clothes, drenching me. Fear combined with the chill to leach away my body heat.

"I bet your meat will be quite tender," she cooed. "All I need to do is thrust in my fangs to wet my throat with that beautiful blood of yours, like a sweet drink of fine sake." The gravelly tone of an old woman intertwined with the sultry notes of a seductress. She patted my cheeks, neck, collarbones, and elsewhere, robbing me of yet more heat.

"N-no!" I let out a shrill scream and tried to crawl away, though I had little hope of actually escaping her clutches. Goosebumps covered my body. My hands and feet refused to respond properly. Even still, I struggled, desperate to escape the cold death that awaited me. More and more soil was forced up under my fingernails each time I scratched my hands into the ground for purchase, but I got no farther.

The woman cackled. "Ah, I see we have a lively one."

She seemed overjoyed to watch me struggle. Something wrapped tightly around my left leg and all my forward movement came to a stop: another silver thread.

"Hnngh!" It was only a matter of time until she caught up to me. I scratched at my leg to release the thread, but it held firm, biting into my skin and refusing to break. Then something soft pressed down on me.

"Oh, can't run away anymore?" the woman smirked as all

eight of her legs straddled me. The moonlight grew just a little bit brighter, as though the spider were glowing. Her skin was as pale as a corpse. Wet, black hair clung to her face and body. She wore a scarlet kimono that may once have been a prized piece but was now tattered and dirt-stained. With no obi to hold the kimono closed at her waist, or undershirt to cover her body, her round breasts and navel were completely exposed. Around her hips, she changed from a woman to a spider with a striped abdomen and eight long legs covered with fine hairs.

This was Jorogumo. This was the same figure drawn by Toriyama Sekien, the figure of the Tsukumogami who'd come to life.

Jorogumo gave her head a playful shake and curled her blood-red lips into a smile. A strange clicking sound came from somewhere; it took me several seconds to realize that it was the sound of my own teeth chattering. Caged by her eight legs, caught in the grip and pinned by the gaze of this pale, half-naked woman, I quaked with terror.

Jorogumo's black eyes widened, as if she were basking in my fear. "What a beautiful little child you are. And now I shall eat you. That's great news, isn't it?"

Her cackling stopped just as suddenly as it started. In the next moment, she was baring her sharp fangs, thick liquid dripping from the points.

It was all over for me.

Just as I resigned myself to my fate, someone dove in and kicked Jorogumo. They slammed her back and cast some kind of spell, throwing an ofuda-like paper talisman right at Jorogumo's exposed stomach. On contact, the paper disintegrated like ash, eliciting a pained scream from the Tsukumogami.

"Kaori, are you okay?" Suimei was looking down at me, his face pale. He turned his back on Jorogumo, who was still writhing in agony, and cut the silver thread around my leg with a knife. Then he hefted me up and took off running.

"Whoa, so you're going to carry me off like a princess now?" I gasped "Where are we going?"

"We're running away. Unfortunately, my attack was only strong enough to slow her down. Like I told you, I'm not an exorcist right now, so we'll have to leave the rest up to your family."

Suimei ran along the river with Jorogumo fast on our heels. Spiders poured out of the wound in her torn belly. "I won't forgive you!" she shrieked. "I won't forgive you, filthy humans!"

"Gah, just shut up, lady..."

Someone appeared right in Jorogumo's path. It was the spirit who had watched over me my whole life, the "peculiar" man who was the most reliable and caring person I knew, the one who'd taken me in when I was at my most vulnerable. Shinonome-san cracked his neck and rolled up his sleeves.

"Don't think I'm just going to overlook what you've done, you Tsukumogami impostor!" he roared.

The scales covering Shinonome-san's cheeks flared. More scales fanned out over his entire body, and he started to glow turquoise. His nails extended into fierce claws, his exposed canines grew razor sharp, and his bluish-gray eyes let off a golden light as he fixed them on Jorogumo.

Shinonome-san launched toward his opponent.

Jorogumo merely smiled. "Interesting—I suppose I'll eat you instead."

"Heh, just try it!"

The Hirose River glimmered in the moonlight, the shadows of the two combatants reflecting on its surface. Columns of water shot high up into the air, raining down over the surrounding area as Shinonome-san and Jorogumo clashed atop the river. More explosions roared in the distance as the raven twins jumped into the fray.

I just wanted everyone to come out of this safely. Suimei set me down, and I sat there watching the flurry of violence from a distance, helpless.

Suddenly, Noname grabbed my arm. "Kaori, we don't have time to watch this. Let's go!"

"S-sorry," I stammered.

"Nyaa-san, take us to that thing's nest," said Noname.

"Got it!"

I hurried after Noname as Nyaa-san led us to a grassy spot right next to the deep pool in the river. Countless silver threads wrapped around a dead tree, forming a large nest. Noname inspected the threads until she found something rolling around in the deepest part of it. From there, she extracted something just large enough to hold in her arms. The legs of some kind of black beast protruded from gaps in the silver thread bound around it.

"Kuro?!" Suimei rushed over and tore away the threads.

Noname and I leapt in to help. It took some time, but we finally got him out.

A spirit that looked like a cross between a dog and a weasel emerged from the tangle. Red spots marked his black fur. He was exactly as Suimei had described him.

Even freed from the thread, Kuro just lay there, eyes closed. Foam collected at the corners of his mouth. Could it be—

"He's been weakened by the spider's venom," Noname confirmed. "We can't treat him here. Let's take him home."

"But what about Shinonome-san and the others?" I asked anxiously.

"You can leave the dirty work to them. We have to do what we can." Noname turned to Suimei. "Well, Suimei-chan? This is your partner, isn't it? I'll take care of the healing, but it's your job to be there by his side when he finally awakens."

Suimei blanched. "But I..."

"I don't know what you're so uncertain about, but is it really more important than his life?" Noname scolded.

Suimei hesitated before finally shaking his head and picking up Kuro. "Let's go, then. Please help him."

"Of course." Noname smiled. "Just leave it to me."

Suimei studied his friend with melancholy eyes.

Noname set a hand on his shoulder. "It's okay. I'm sure we've made it in time. Anyway, aren't they going a little overboard over there?"

Fwoosh!

Another large column of water shot up out of the river. Noname averted her gaze and muttered something about how there would be a big to-do about this the following morning, but that had little to do with us. And with that, she hurried us all away.

Upon returning to the spirit realm, we immediately headed for Noname's shop. Suimei laid Kuro on a bed so Noname could wipe his blood-drenched fur clean with a towel. Fortunately, Kuro hadn't suffered many deep wounds. Rather, it seemed that he had mostly just been weakened by the venom injected into his body.

"Luckily, I have an antidote. The rest is all just physical trauma, so we'll need some ointment for that. Now, the ingredients... Suimei?" Noname began to request various items only for her eyes to widen as Suimei headed her off by handing her everything she needed.

"I have some knowledge of Chinese medicines," he said. "Let me help."

Noname smiled. "Then we'll also need some—"

"Got it."

I had no idea what those two were doing, so I stood in the corner and tried to stay out of the way. I hated feeling so useless, but there was nothing more I could do. They were the experts here.

Finally, Noname remembered me and pointed at the kitchen. "Can you make some rice and throw together a bunch of onigiri? Those boys will be starving after that big fight."

"Right!" I leapt to the task, eager to be helpful.

Two hours and some very intense work on Kuro later, everyone slumped down, exhausted.

We took a break for tea and snacks. The sweetness of the treats dissolved the exhaustion weighing down my limbs. Nyaasan, who'd dozed off while we were all hard at work, sat on my lap eating dried sardines. Oh, to live as carefree as a cat.

Kuro snored gently in the bed. It seemed he'd finally stabilized after his ordeal.

Noname sighed with relief. "I'm so relieved it worked out. Spiders inject venom into their prey to prevent them from moving, then they inject digestive juices to dissolve their prey's innards into a slush to eat. It was almost too late."

"Wow, now I'm scared of spiders." I shivered.

Noname shrugged. "It's just their way. In any case, Kuro should wake up soon. I'm going to put on some more tea; just wait a bit."

While Noname headed to the kitchen with the empty teapot, I turned my attention to the sleeping Kuro. Even ignoring his injuries, Kuro was quite thin. His ribs protruded alarmingly at his sides.

"Kuro..." Suimei said, frowning at his companion.

Just as Suimei reached out to touch the animal, Kuro's eyes blinked open. He looked around in confusion "Sui...mei?" His expression changed in a flash; Kuro bared his fangs and growled. "Don't touch me."

Kuro staggered to his feet. He glared at Suimei with bloodshot eyes. However, the effect of the venom hadn't entirely worn off, and he wavered where he stood.

"Can't I at least worry about you?" Suimei pleaded.

"No!" Kuro drew back farther, right off the edge of the bed. He let out a startled cry as he hit the floor.

"Kuro!"

Suimei rushed to Kuro and pulled him close, cradling his friend's light body in his arms.

"No, stop it!" Kuro thrashed in his hold. "I don't need you anymore! Don't look at me...don't touch me...don't hold me!"

"Calm down, you're going to make yourself sick." Suimei scratched behind Kuro's ears as he whispered to him.

"No, stop...oh, oh! There...oh, oh! That feels good!" Kuro moaned, tail wagging.

"That was a bit too easy, wasn't it?" I mused.

"No, it wasn't!" Kuro snarled. "Just stop it, don't be so kind to me. Don't you hate me?"

No matter how Kuro protested, Suimei just went on gazing at him softly. Whatever had happened in their past, it seemed they could never truly hate each other.

I stroked Nyaa-san on my lap, enjoying the rumble of her purring. It seemed to me that Suimei and Kuro probably had a similar relationship. It'd be a real tragedy if they didn't get past this disagreement.

As I thought that, I recalled Suimei's words from earlier: *Can you forgive someone who ate your parents?* Had Kuro really done something like that? Feeling my curious gaze, Kuro's ears perked up to sharp points.

"Hey, did something happen to make you get all stubborn and reject Suimei?" I asked. "Can you tell me about it?"

Kuro cast his gaze downward.

"I can explain," Suimei offered.

"Are you sure?" Kuro asked.

"It's fine. After all, you've done a lot for me." Suimei continued to stroke Kuro's back as he spoke: "Kuro and I have been together ever since I was little. Considering I always had to suppress my emotions, having Kuro around was a huge boon to me. He was the only one with whom I could escape my daily life and just relax. It's thanks to Kuro that I've been an exorcist this long. We weren't just partners—we were friends."

Kuro remained silent, curled up in Suimei's arms.

Suimei's eyes took on a distant look as he continued. "One day, Kuro suddenly disappeared. Under normal circumstances, an Inugami can't stay separated very long from the partner they've bonded with, but he destroyed my mother's tombstone in order to gain his freedom. What's more...he ate her bones."

My eyes widened. "He did what?"

"Do you know how Inugami are made, Kaori?"

They and other tsukimono could be created in a variety of different ways. For generations, Suimei's family had done it like this: They buried a dog in the ground up to its neck. Then, when the animal was on the verge of starvation, they threw its favorite treat toward it. The moment the dog craned its neck toward the treat, they lopped its head off with a sword, which they burned so that they could then carry the newly forged Inugami's skull as a sign of its binding. It was all terribly cruel.

"Kuro is an Inugami created by the first generation of my clan," Suimei said. "In the past, we used to have other Inugami as well, but now only Kuro remains. When an Inugami is attached to a tsukimono clan, his spirit is anchored to their bones. The only way he could break the binding would be to eat the bones of someone from the line that created him—my family's line. Though even I didn't know that until recently."

His expression grew complicated. "I have a poor relationship with my father. My mother is the only person in my family I'd ever try to forgive. ...And Kuro ate her bones. Even though she was such an important person to me."

In the Shirai household, Suimei had had no other allies but Kuro, not since he lost the one relative he held dear—his mother. All in the same horrible day, Suimei found his best friend missing and his mother's grave desecrated. In one fell swoop, he lost the two things that were most important to him.

Suimei stared at nothing as he continued in a mumble. "Listen, Kuro, if you had to eat someone, then it should have been me. Not only would that have left my mother alone, but it would have been quite the curse to place on my family. If you wanted to be free, I would have accepted that. I'd gladly sacrifice myself for you."

Kuro stared at Suimei as he spoke but said nothing.

Nyaa-san, who'd been silent up until that moment, finally raised her head. "Hey, Kaori. What's everyone so worked up over?"

She truly had the social graces of a cat.

Suimei jerked his head up. "What do you mean, cat?"

"You really don't know?" Nyaa-san asked. Suddenly, a bright red flame erupted from her body. The fire shimmered and wrapped around me, since she was still in my arms. I didn't get burned, though. Nyaa-san ensured I felt no more than a tickle. "I'm a Kasha, you know. I wonder if I ever told you that. It's a type of spirit who takes both the living and the dead to hell. My favorite food is human corpses."

Nyaa-san smiled as she licked her front paws clean. "Fish is good, too, but there's something to be said about the taste of a human. It's hard to express in words."

Suimei narrowed his eyes. "Are you saying Kuro ate my mother's bones because they tasted good?! Don't be ridiculous. Kuro doesn't eat people!"

I startled at the sudden surge of emotion from him. Nyaa-san had really hit a sore spot.

"Wait until I'm done talking or you'll misunderstand what I'm trying to say," Nyaa-san sniffed. "There are two reasons why I eat humans. One is that they're delicious. The other is..."

Nyaa-san leaped through the air to land on Suimei's shoulder. She leaned in close to Kuro, who flattened his ears and drew his tail between his legs.

"You liked her, didn't you?" Nyaa-san asked.

"Eep!" Kuro buried his nose in Suimei's armpit, shaking head to tail.

"Well, you've got a cute voice, at least. Teasing you could be fun." Nyaa-san deliberately stomped on Kuro as she stepped down from Suimei's shoulder. She didn't even bother to look back as Kuro let out a yelp of pain, and she returned to my lap.

"The more I like a person, the more I want to eat them, especially after they die," Nyaa-san said. "I gobble down their intestines, gnaw on their bones, lap up their blood. It helps me keep the memory of them in my heart. Of course, that all goes out the window when I'm hungry." Nyaa-san stood up on my lap and rubbed her face against mine. "I'm supposed to get Kaori's corpse when she dies."

"What?!" Suimei stared.

"That's right," I said, stroking Nyaa-san. "Eat it clean and don't let anything go to waste."

"Sure thing!" Nyaa-san purred. "I'll take my time to savor every last bite. You know, kind of like a memorial service."

Suimei stared at me, stunned, as I smiled at the prospect of being eaten by my closest companion.

"Eating bones might seem like a betrayal among humans, but it has the exact opposite meaning for spirits," I said. "Suimei, did you and Kuro ever have a proper discussion about this?"

Suimei narrowed his eyes and did not respond.

I brought my cheek down to rub against Nyaa-san's purring head. "Of course, even if spirits like to eat the corpse of someone they love, it's different if they don't have permission. Mutual consent makes the act more meaningful. There must be a reason for that. The time that humans and spirits can spend together may seem long to us, but it's actually quite short to them. It'd be a waste to spend your limited time together misunderstanding each other."

In this vast world, getting to meet a person you think is important is so incredibly valuable. If that person is a spirit, you should spare no effort trying to work things out with them.

"Hey, Suimei," I went on, "Let's sit down and talk this through. If you just keep holding it in, nothing will change. If you keep your eyes closed, you'll miss something important."

I hugged Nyaa-san against me, smiling at the feel of her warm fur. "Humans and spirits really can get along, I promise. You just have to talk things through."

While Suimei hesitated, Nyaa-san thrashed in my hold.

"Auuugh! Kaori, you're squeezing me too tight!"

"Oh, sorry!"

"I'm always telling you to ease up! When I want to be held, I'll come to you, okay? So try to not be so aggressive."

"You're a real handful, you know that?"

Nyaa-san slipped through my arms and dashed off. Well, so much for my hands-on demonstration. I worried the lesson might have been ruined, but then I heard laughter bubbling up. Suimei's shoulders shook, and his face scrunched up into a smile. This was the first time I'd ever seen him look so carefree.

Kuro looked up at him and snorted. "It seems like you've changed, my friend. Or, rather, maybe someone has changed you. Now you can get angry. You can even laugh..." Kuro rolled out of Suimei's arms and landed on the floor. He gazed right into my eyes. "All right, I suppose I should talk. About why I left my partner's side and the stupid choices I made."

Kuro's tail swished in irritation. "My oldest memory is of a man staring at me, mocking me as I lie on the ground." He glanced up at Suimei. "That was your ancestor, the original head of the Shirai family."

A tsukimono can bring immense wealth to its clan. After acquiring vast wealth thanks to their Inugami, the first generation of the Shirai family started working as exorcists to hunt spirits. Kuro's owner continued to hunt spirits in exchange for vast sums of money, all the while continuing to abuse Kuro.

"There were a lot of Inugami besides myself at the time, but... well, they all died," Kuro said. "A consequence of working with exorcists. I managed to push on, and before I knew it, I was the only one left. Then I got a new master..."

That master was a young girl with curious eyes who wore a peony-patterned kimono. Midori—Suimei's mother.

"Midori beamed the moment we met," Kuro said, "though she was quickly scolded for that. Her smile was like a ray of sunshine. I can still see it even now."

She had treated Kuro with incredible kindness. Whereas Kuro's prior masters had treated him like a disposable tool, she treated him like family. She especially liked his black fur and would often run her hands through it. The simple pleasure of the touch had shocked Kuro after years of overwork—but it had brought him great relief.

"Up until that time, I'd loathed the Shirai family for turning me into an Inugami, but her kindness helped me move past my bitterness." Kuro's tail went on wagging, but no longer in irritation. "And unlike the previous heads of the family, Midori had no interest in making any more Inugami. She was far too kind, and she hated the cruel practice. Though she was under a lot of pressure from the rest of the clan, she stubbornly refused."

Kuro saw the rest of the Shirai family as nothing but parasites who wanted more of the wealth an Inugami would bring. "They worked Midori and me to the bone, all the while despising me. However, Midori had the strength to resist them."

Then, when she was grown, she had a baby.

"An adorable, round little baby boy who cried with such vigor," Kuro said fondly. "He really was the cutest."

Yet Suimei bowed his head with some silent feeling.

"Once Suimei was born, Midori's health took a turn for the worse," Kuro went on. "The once strong young woman was now completely bedridden, her days as an exorcist over. She had never much cared for the job, however. Near the end, all she wanted was to spend her time with me and Suimei."

Then one day, she spoke to Kuro while they watched over her sleeping baby: *Being born into this clan, one bound to a tsukimono, means I must suppress all of my emotions. I suppose that's just my fate. Envy will only lead to disaster, after all. But I don't want to see this child's smile snuffed out like mine was. I want him to grow up healthy and full of emotion. What mother wouldn't want that for her child?*

"Midori didn't look like a girl anymore as she said this... In that moment, she truly had the face of a mother. It was so beautiful. I may have fallen in love in that moment. I swore to myself that I would never forget what she said to me that day." Kuro sighed. "Then, when Suimei turned three, the Shirai family began his education—mostly led by his father."

Just like his mother, he was forced to learn how to suppress his emotions and kill spirits.

"I hated it," Kuro said. "I hated that he couldn't live like a normal boy. Suimei was a very kind child, just like Midori. And that only made it all the more unbearable to watch that family try to break him. Suimei had to suppress his emotions because of me. Then again, I also wanted him to grow up into a strong, functional adult. The mere existence of the Inugami had cursed his bloodline; whether I wanted to or not was irrelevant. I felt conflicted about the whole thing."

The power that bound a tsukimono to their clan was irrevocable.

Kuro shook his head. "I thought about it for a long time, but what could I do? Then one day, a visitor came to see Midori. A human man with a disconcerting gaze. He claimed there was a way to release me. But I would have to eat the bones of my master. I shuddered at the very idea. How could I eat Midori?

"That man, he just smiled at my horror and said, 'Well, she need not be alive. After she dies, then you can eat her bones. Even if it won't set your current master free, at least the next generation will be saved. Don't you want that boy to be able to smile again?'"

I couldn't really argue with that, but it still sounded odd.

"The strange man just kept going, though. 'It's perfectly normal for a spirit to want to eat the bones of someone they like,'

he said. 'It's just like a memorial service. A perfectly normal memorial service. Nothing wrong with it at all.'"

Kuro sniffed. "Of course, I wasn't just going to accept something like that. When pushed, the man said I couldn't just eat
the bones of her predecessor. I had to eat the bones of someone
I truly loved. ...Naturally, I was suspicious of all this, so I asked
the man what he wanted, why he'd come here and offered this
information. He just smiled and said, 'I love watching old things
break.'"

Kuro shuddered at the memory before he continued.
"Everything about it was so strange that I just figured that he was
lying to us or something. But when Midori passed on and the
Shirai family put even more pressure on Suimei, I couldn't help
remembering his words."

Any time the young Suimei showed emotion back then, his
family would shove him into a dark, cramped room without
enough space to even stand. If he cried or got sick, they would
only scold him even more. It got so excessive that his dark hair,
inherited from his mother, turned silvery gray.

"There is no limit to human greed," Kuro said. "I don't think
I could ever put a little child through such torture in the name of
discipline. I was so scared of them, but I wanted to rescue Suimei."

Kuro fretted for a long time over what to do.

"If I ate Midori's bones, Suimei would be released from the
tsukimono possession. But it would mean we would have to part
ways. And there was no chance he'd forgive me for eating his
mother's bones. I didn't even think I could forgive myself."

Worse, by then Suimei had seemed so dependent on Kuro. The life had almost completely drained from his eyes. He cried any time Kuro left, even if he only went a short distance. He worried that Suimei would shatter completely.

But he remained, watching over Suimei until he was old enough to stand on his own two feet. Once he believed Suimei could make it on his own, he would release them both from that horrible life.

One night, after Suimei turned seventeen, Kuro finally put his plan into action. He cried as he dug up Midori-san's grave and ate her bones, apologizing the whole time. But there was no one to hear. He was alone, crunching on the bones of the woman he'd loved so much, locking the hurt away deep inside himself.

"Midori's bones...they were delicious. I was full of pain, sorrow, and regret as I did it, but I was also glad that she could become part of me." Kuro paused and looked up at Suimei with his round, dog-like eyes. Tears rolled down his face. "I'm sorry. I really am. I ran away because I just couldn't face you after that. But I don't regret it. That smile on your face, it reminds me of the smile I saw on Midori's so many years ago. It turns out the man was telling the truth. What I did that night truly did release you from me. I'm glad, I really am. Now I can tell Midori the good news."

"Tell...her?" Suimei said.

Suddenly, Kuro spun around and dashed out of the shop.

"Kuro!" Suimei called.

"Wait!" I called after.

We rushed out of the shop and found Kuro in the middle of

the road, where he'd apparently run out of strength. Glimmerflies swept in when Suimei and I stumbled out, brightening the perpetual gloom.

"Where were you going?" Suimei demanded.

Kuro gaped at the glimmerflies. "These insects...are they glimmerflies? I only just learned of them, after having lived in the human world for so long...but I feel like I can relate. I don't really feel all that close to other spirits. But I find myself drawn to humans, just like them."

A veritable swarm had gathered by this point, probably because Suimei and I were there together. The beat of their fluttering wings whispered around us while they illuminated the patch of road where we stood, like the moon shone down only on us.

Kuro smiled faintly. "You know, humans really belong in a world of brightness, never far from light. Spirits are much more suited to aimlessly wriggling around in this darkness."

He looked more relaxed now as he sat down.

"Hey, Suimei," he said. "You know, I've lived my whole life under human protection. But I realized something when we were apart. I can't live alone, I just can't. Look at how thin I've gotten. I don't even know how to make a living for myself so I can eat. Pretty pathetic, isn't it? So anyway, I decided to stop fighting it and just wait patiently for my end to come. I have no regrets, though. I'm going to die and finally achieve my sweet release. With that, Suimei will be able to live in a bright, happy world. You can laugh when you want and cry as you please. And someday...I hope you can forgive me."

Kuro glanced over his shoulder at us. "It really does hurt for you to keep on hating me, Suimei. So...please..."

Once more, Kuro started away, leaving a stunned Suimei behind.

I burst from the swarm of glimmerflies and chased after Kuro. I grabbed him by the scruff of the neck and gave him a shake, then tossed him in Suimei's direction.

"Hyaugh?!" he cried.

"Kuro!"

Kuro flipped through the air and landed easily in Suimei's arms. Pretty good throw, if I did say so myself—though my hands were still trembling despite my bravado.

"Hey, what's this about?!" Kuro demanded. "You're going to hurt my back, whipping my long body around like that! Be more careful!"

I just planted my feet and crossed my arms under my chest. "Shut up, you!"

"Huh?!"

I jabbed a finger at Kuro as he trembled with fear and burrowed his nose into Suimei's armpit.

"You're acting like the victim here, but you don't deserve any pity."

Kuro tensed.

"C'mon, it's painfully obvious that you still want to stay with him," I said. "If that's what you want, then do it. If you want to live together with Suimei, then just say it!"

"But!" He hesitated, fumbling for words. "Spirits and humans are naturally different, absolutely incompatible. Could we really tolerate one another? If you were bound to something so different from yourself, you'd only end up exhausted. It would be challenging, frustrating—painful, even." Kuro shook his head, expression conflicted. Then he looked curiously at me. "Hey, why are you crying?"

I sniffled.

No matter how much I wiped my eyes, the tears just kept coming. I'd worked so hard to get Suimei to admit I was an adult, and now I was standing there bawling like a baby. But Kuro's words were just too heart-wrenching for me to bear.

"Don't speak in absolutes," I insisted. "I don't believe humans and spirits are so incompatible."

Kuro didn't know it, but his words essentially rejected my whole life up until this point. I loved and cherished all the spirits I lived with. Maybe I caused them a lot of trouble, but they'd helped raise me, and I adored them for that. I was glad that I'd been lost in this strange world, even if I did sometimes feel out of place.

A giant, unknown spirit had left me petrified. The spirits around me had been fine while I was terrified, and it had been overwhelming to realize just how different human and spirit sensibilities could be.

On the other hand, there were the small spirits, those with minuscule life spans. I just couldn't quite bring myself to reconcile with the idea that they would return with their fragile bodies fading away in my arms.

And then there was me. I didn't want to make the spirits who cared about me sad. I was destined to die one day. To leave them.

It would be so painful. Was it really okay for me to impose on them? I was human, after all. There was no helping that, no matter what I wanted.

The glimmerflies that had temporarily fluttered off returned. I wanted to hide in the darkness like everyone else—but they wouldn't allow it. I'd always be a misfit here. The glimmerflies trailed me everywhere, marking me out as a tumor, a foreign body who didn't belong.

That's why I had to say these things to the confused and frightened Kuro. I wanted to dispel the anxiety that swirled within him. If neither humans nor spirits were "absolute" then neither could be incompatible with the other.

"It's going to be okay," I said. "We can still understand one another. That's what I believe."

I was still crying, my chest clenching around the flow of tears. I wished I could run away and not have to face this conflict I'd contended with for my entire life, but if I remained silent, Kuro might make a horrible mistake. I pushed on, yelling now.

"If you think you've done something unforgivable, then don't give up until you're forgiven! It doesn't matter if you're a human or spirit, that's true for everyone. Being together, that's the most important thing. But it's not everything..."

I wanted to be with Shinonome-san, even knowing that I would someday become an old woman. I wanted to be his daughter forever. I wanted to live here in this world until the end of my days. The tears clogged my throat, preventing me from continuing. I hid my face in my hands, wishing I could let it all out somehow, but no matter how hard I cried, more tears kept coming. I wanted to force down all my built-up emotions into the tears that kept pouring down my cheeks—to get them all out of me. Even if I knew they would just build up all over again. This was no true solution.

Then someone gently wiped the dampness off my cheek.

"Thank you." It was Suimei.

He then stepped away from me to lift Kuro into his arms, holding him at eye level. "This is the first time I've ever heard about what my mother said to you. I had no idea that eating her was a mourning practice for spirits. I was so angry with you because I thought you had defiled her."

"Had I said anything to you, you would have been conflicted," Kuro said. "I didn't want to be a burden."

"But I wanted to know these things. I wish I'd known sooner. Dammit." Anger washed across Suimei's face. He pressed his forehead against Kuro's, tears tracking down his cheeks and soaking into Kuro's fur. "I don't forgive you."

"What?"

"You want me to forgive you, don't you? Well, I can't do that right away. I still haven't had a chance to come to terms with the fact that you ate my mother. I want you to stay with me, so when the day comes that I *can* forgive you, we'll be together. I'm going to try really hard to do that, so please, stay with me." Suimei sniffled, voice trembling. "Maybe I've grown bigger, but I'm still a good-for-nothing kid who can't do anything without you. Just as you can't live alone, neither can I."

The overt show of emotion almost made him look like a child again. After so long suppressing his feelings, he was clumsy, and his face scrunched up terribly, and it was clear that to Kuro, this display came as a shock. For the first time since coming here, Suimei was being completely honest as he laid his feelings bare.

Kuro trembled before he let out a delighted cry. He leaned in and licked Suimei's nose, nuzzling against his face. Suimei smiled back, eyes wet with tears.

"Hey, maybe we can stay together forever, then," Kuro said.

Suimei blinked for a moment before he broke out into laughter. "Of course we can! We're friends, aren't we?"

Kuro excitedly licked Suimei's face, tail wagging frantically. Suimei, his face now sticky and covered in drool, protested that it tickled.

I felt warm just watching them. From now on, Suimei would be able to live with his emotions, just as Midori-san had wished.

I turned, wanting to give them some privacy for their reunion, only to find someone charging toward me.

"Kaori, something bad's happened!" Shinonome-san shouted. He was covered in sweat and threw me under his arm the moment he reached me.

"Aaack! What are you doing?!" I yelped.

"No time to talk! Nyaa, where are you? I need you to carry Kaori so we can get going!" Nyaa-san, who had a bright red, sniffly nose for some strange reason, stepped out of the apothecary with Noname beside her.

"What's wrong?" Noname frowned. "You need to calm down this instant."

"Oh, no...wh-wh-what happened?!" Nyaa-san demanded.

As soon as Noname saw Shinonome-san's face, she went pale as a sheet. "You didn't let Jorogumo get away, did you?!"

Shinonome-san shook his head. "No, no, I've got her cornered well enough, but we haven't been able to defeat her."

"Hey!" Noname scolded. "That spider becomes fixated on its prey the moment it sets its eyes on it! You don't think it's coming here, do you?! Kill it, you idiot!"

"I'm just a bookstore owner!"

Noname groaned and headed back into her shop to find a weapon. Shinonome-san refocused on the enlarged Nyaa-san.

"Run away as far as you can," he instructed. "If this place gets destroyed, then I fear for the rest of us."

"I'm pretty sure Noname is the one you'd have to worry about if you got the whole town destroyed," Nyaa-san said.

"True enough. When she gets really angry, she's scarier than King Enma on a power trip."

"Killing spiders, huh?" Suimei asked. "I'd like to join."

I turned to him in shock. "Suimei?! What are you talking about?!"

"Killing spiders is no easy task," Shinonome-san warned. "Leave it to us professionals."

"Don't push yourself," I said to Suimei. "Kuro is still weak, you know."

"Thank you for your concern," Kuro said. "But with my partner back at my side, I've got the strength of one hundred spirits. Right, Suimei?"

Suimei grinned. "That's right, Kuro."

The pair nodded at each other. Despite a slight limp, Kuro looked sturdy and determined, his tail tall.

Suimei dug in a pouch at his waist and pulled out a medicine bottle, from which he poured a white object that he presented to his friend. "Kuro, this is yours."

"Don't be stupid," Kuro sniffed. "Without that, I won't be of any use to you."

"And that's why I'm giving it to you. We are no longer master and tsukimono. Like I said, we're friends."

Kuro smiled, even as a fresh tear tracked down his cheek. "Thank you."

Suimei was presenting Kuro with the skull that had created him. Kuro accepted it and swallowed it whole. A moment later, his hair stood on end. His body shifted, filling out, fur thickening. It was like this one missing piece of himself had added some sort of crucial vitality to his whole body. He shuddered excitedly and snuggled up to Suimei, who gave a satisfied nod at the sight of the change.

"Suimei!" I called after him. "Please, be careful."

"It's okay," he assured me. "I won't let Jorogumo go, not after what she did to Kuro. Oh, and..." Suimei's eyes crinkled as he smiled brightly in my direction. "Thank you so much. You really helped a lot."

That gentle smile...it was so unfamiliar on him. Seeing it from so close made my heart race.

"I'll be back!" he said, rushing off with Kuro.

I slumped on Nyaa-san's back as the light of the glimmerflies faded away.

"Feels like spring," Nyaa-san remarked. But I could read the undercurrent of her words, the suggestion behind her teasing tone. Spring was the season in which love bloomed.

She dashed away down the streets. Even pursued by spiders, I couldn't help but grin. Somehow, I just felt that everything would turn out okay.

Two hours later, news reached us where we were hiding out in the mountains that Suimei and the others had successfully captured Jorogumo and saved our home.

Living in the Spirit Realm

I GENTLY SQUEEZED the brilliant white rice so as not to crush the individual grains as I added the standard ingredients: boiled kelp, salmon, pollock roe, and pickled plums. And one special twist.

"This is amazing! Fried chicken and eggs, yum!" Kuro cheered.

"Pretty good, huh?" I said. "I made it special for Shinonome-san since he's such a lazy bum."

"You know, this is the first time I've ever eaten something so delicious," Kuro mused.

"Whoa, Kuro, slow down a bit or you're going to choke. Hey, there's rice stuck in your fur."

Suimei just watched, smiling at his partner. Together, the two of them had played a major role in capturing Jorogumo. And a good thing they had too. Had we let the Tsukumogami copy of the ferocious Jorogumo run free, she could have harmed far more people. With no police force in the spirit realm, an attack like that tended to turn into every spirit for themselves.

It wasn't just Suimei and Kuro who'd dashed off to thwart Jorogumo, to be clear. When word spread that I was the target, the bookstore's regulars had rushed in to help. I wanted to think they hadn't killed her, but the terrifying look on Umi Zato's face as he'd run off to join the fray made me wonder.

"Don't do anything too scary, okay?" I'd said at the time.

"You've got nothing to worry about," Umi Zato said. "We're just going to make sure that she doesn't want to see any more humans for quite a while."

They most certainly had.

Now, Shinonome-san brooded quietly over his miso soup. At times like this, it was best to just leave him alone.

I sipped my own ginger-infused miso. At least Noname was in a good mood, unlike my pouty father.

"Jorogumo's silver silk threads are quite rare," she sang. "I managed to get quite a few, and now I can make some clothes out of them. Maybe you and I can have matching outfits, Kaori."

Noname was mesmerized by the glittering silver thread. She flipped through a kimono catalog, plotting how to spin the threads into wondrous attire—though she looked a bit disappointed with whatever she was finding.

"Oh," she said, looking up. "Suimei-chan, Kuro-chan, I meant to ask: Do you have anywhere you can stay now? If you don't, you should come live with me. My house may be a little small for Kuro-chan, but Suimei-chan, you know a lot about medicine, right? I'd love it if you could help with my apothecary work. Things get pretty busy in the summer with all the idiots running wild."

Suimei shot me a look. He was currently using our guest room, as he had been before. Ordinarily, we loaned it out to customers visiting from far away. Otherwise it just sat empty.

Though I'd be a bit lonely, I nodded at him. Suimei looked at Kuro and some silent agreement passed between them.

"All right," Kuro said. "Now I'll have a sweet little auntie to look after me."

Everyone went absolutely still. Though Noname's face didn't change, rage flared just under the surface.

"Eh...he he...he... Ignorance sure can be terrifying, can't it?" Kinme muttered.

"You'd best take that back unless you want her to rub mustard in your wounds," Ginme advised.

Though the twins were deathly pale, Kuro just tilted his head to the side. "Hmm, big sister, then?" he suggested.

"Oh, my! I love it." Noname's whole demeanor abruptly changed. "You're going to be my little baby from now on." She pulled Kuro in close and rubbed her cheek against his.

The power of a purehearted doggy truly cannot be underestimated.

Suimei, meanwhile, stared off blankly, barely registering the scene before him. Perhaps he was just tired, but it was a bit eerie, almost like back when we'd first met.

Suddenly, I remembered his smile from not so long ago—just before he and Kuro ran off to deal with Jorogumo.

Thank you so much. You really helped a lot.

A flush crawled up my face. I slapped my hands against my

cheeks to relieve the heat but to no avail. My heart tried to pound right out of my chest.

What was happening to me? I dared to glance back at Suimei. The moment my eyes met his perfect hazel gaze, my heart started to race all over again.

"Hey, Kaori?" he said.

"What?" Aaah! My voice cracked!

While I was busy trying to get myself under control, Suimei mumbled under his breath, "Kuro is really adorable."

"Huh?" I said.

"That black coat," he said. "The way his skull rounds off in the back, his long torso and short feetsies..."

"Feetsies..." I could hardly believe what I was hearing.

"It feels amazing to pet him," Suimei went on. "And he even knows how to wait properly if you give him the command. You can hold out his favorite beef jerky, and he'll just wait there so patiently. What a smart pup..."

"Smart..."

I let my gaze unfocus as I listened to Suimei rave about Kuro's charms. His love warmed every word, as though Kuro was the very heart and soul of Suimei's being.

After the incident with Jorogumo, Suimei and Kuro had decided to leave the exorcism business. It was impossible to make a new contract now that Kuro's body had been returned to him, anyway. Plus, with the tsukimono binding now lifted, Suimei's emotions no longer needed to be suppressed.

Nevertheless, the two of them would always be together now.

They would live together as one unit, just a human and a spirit together as friends. I was confident that Suimei and Kuro would build a wonderful life side by side. They might run into challenges, but they would overcome them, I was sure of it.

Nyaa-san hopped up on my lap and nosed against my hand for attention. She mumbled under her breath as I stroked her fur. "Aww, the breakfast table will be awfully empty without Suimei around."

"Huh?"

"Are you stupid? With Suimei gone, we won't get any rent. Say goodbye to all this great rice."

"Oh, right... Well, I'm fine with the cheap stuff. I can just go back to it." I looked down at the brilliant white rice, already mourning its loss, before abruptly turning back to Suimei. No, actually, I *couldn't* go back to the cheap stuff. It was intolerable. I got on my hands and knees to grovel, big wet tears forming at the corners of my eyes.

"Please, Suimei, stay with us a little longer," I begged. "What about two more months? Is that okay?"

Alas, I was rejected outright.

"Why? I'm going to live at the apothecary with Kuro now," he said.

"I, umm, well...what if only Kuro goes, and you..."

"Are you kidding? You know I'm not going to have the same kind of cash I did before. In fact, I need to tighten my belt and live frugally here in the spirit realm. Although I do intend to cash out all my assets in the human world. Man, I wonder how the rest of the clan will look then. They've probably been shaking since they realized their Inugami was gone." Suimei smirked darkly and cackled. "The home the Inugami abandoned will now fall into ruin. Too bad!"

"That's mean!" I said. I'd never seen this darker side of Suimei before.

Someone patted my shoulder. Shinonome-san thrust his thumb up into the air. "We'll figure it out together, as father and daughter."

"But this is all your fault to begin with," I moaned. "If you actually took money when you lent out books, I wouldn't need a part-time job!"

How oblivious could he be?

I batted at him in annoyance, but he just laughed and dodged away to the other side of the small living room as I lunged after him. Ginme took in the spectacle while Kinme casually sipped at his tea. Nyaa-san just curled up in the corner of the room without a care in the world...and also to avoid getting involved. Suimei continued to smile at Kuro as his beloved pet tried to escape Noname's grasp.

I shook my fist at my father. "Gah! You're such an idiot!"

"Oh, really?" He grinned as he danced away again. "With an attitude like that, it's no wonder no one will marry you!"

"Shut up! How can I get married with such a bumbling fool for a father?!"

From then on, my home descended into a familiar chaos. Ah, it was good to be back to normal.

I suddenly stopped short, my gaze drawn to the sky outside the window.

The spirit realm was a world of everlasting night. Though the sun never rose, the sky was filled with stars and an enormous moon. The glimmerflies danced against a swirling backdrop of strange, indescribable colors that washed across the darkened sky.

Spirits ruled this mysterious world. But though it appeared terrifying at first, the spirit realm was home to many gentle and friendly residents. It was the kindest and loveliest place I ever knew. Nothing would ever change that.

Human though I was, I was raised by spirits...and I fully intended to live in their realm today, tomorrow, and every day after that.

Afterword

Greetings, readers old and new alike. My name is Shinobumaru, and I'd like to take a moment to thank you for picking up *The Haunted Bookstore – Gateway to a Parallel Universe*. I'm overjoyed to know that more people can read my story.

From a young age, I always loved stories about spirits from Japanese mythology.

My first exposure to them was in a popular picture book. I was terrified of this horrifying spirit with a giant mouth chomping on salt as it chased after people. Honestly, it was so bad that I couldn't even sleep at night, and yet for some childish reason, I just kept reading the book over and over again.

From there, I read the works of the late Mizuki Shigeru-sensei and Kyogoku Natsuhiko-sensei, which probably contributed to my sense of familiarity with these mythological spirits—even if I'm still terrified that the moment I give them an opening, they might chomp my head off in the dark. They're strange and live at odds with humans, yet I've always felt there was something charming about them. That feeling hasn't changed.

This story is my own take on these mythological spirits.

Seen from Kaori's point of view, the spirit realm is a gentle and beautiful world. However, it's anything but that when taken from Suimei's perspective. To him, it's a visceral, terrifying world where the strong feast on the weak. A lot of my own personal preferences were put into the world inhabited by these spirits.

However, in spite of the world in which they live, I think it's a really heartwarming story. You've got the screwball non-human adoptive father, the affectionate twin birds, the mysterious woman running the apothecary, and of course, the young exorcist boy juggling many issues. I did my best to ensure Kaori and all these other characters felt like they were really alive. I really hope you enjoyed the story right up to the very end.

I received a lot of help in bringing this story to book form. In fact, it's all thanks to one certain individual making an introduction. If I were left to my own devices, there's absolutely no way that this would have ended up in readers' hands as a real product, and for that I'm extremely thankful.

I'd like to thank my editor, Sato, for always providing pointed advice and having a kind word to say. You brought me to tears time and time again with your kind praise.

Munashichi did the cover art. To be completely honest, I had actually been looking at their illustrations while I was writing the story, so I could barely believe Munashichi was actually going to work on this. Having you draw a picture for me was one of my dreams, so I really can't thank you enough.

Finally, I'd like to thank all the designers, proofreaders, marketers, and other people who helped work on this book. Of course, I'd also like to thank my family for supporting me, and you, the reader. I hope we meet again.

Written in the year of the new era
and launch of Kotonoha Bunko,
Shinobumaru